DANNY ORLIS
IN
MYSTERIOUS 'ZANDELAND

*Dedicated to our missionary friends, Earl
and Helena Dix, who made this story possible
by taking us out into the bush in 'Zandeland
where they have served God for more than
thirty years.*

DANNY ORLIS

IN

MYSTERIOUS 'ZANDELAND

BERNARD PALMER

Danny Orlis in Mysterious 'Zandeland
© 2024 by Bernard Palmer
All rights reserved. First edition 1960.
Second edition 2024.

Scripture quotations from The Authorized (King James) Version. Rights in the Authorized Version in the United Kingdom are vested in the Crown. Reproduced by permission of the Crown's patentee, Cambridge University Press.

Cover image: Adobe Firefly
Character illustrations: John Ball
Editor: Charlene Miskimen

Aneko Press Youth

www.anekopress.com

Aneko Press, Life Sentence Publishing, and our logos are trademarks of Life Sentence Publishing, Inc.
203 E. Birch Street
P.O. Box 652
Abbotsford, WI 54405

JUVENILE FICTION / Religious / Christian / Action & Adventure

Paperback ISBN: 978-1-62245-994-0

eBook ISBN: 978-1-62245-995-7

10 9 8 7 6 5 4 3 2 1

Available where books are sold

CONTENTS

CHAPTER 1

AN UNEXPECTED VISITOR

Dan Orlis leaned forward to look out the window of the low-flying DC-3. A panorama of green stretched out below from horizon to horizon, a panorama unbroken by either roads or streams. Only a few dark-red blotches that revealed a handful of newly turned gardens and an occasional brown *sabi*-grass roof scarred the wide expanse of jungle.

All was green below them, a green that was both monotonous and fascinating. Here and there a royal palm thrust its regal fronds above the gently rolling sea of leaves, and a solitary kapok tree reached confidently for the sky.

The jungle seemed peaceful and quiet despite the muffled throbbing of the engines, a strange, majestic, intriguing place.

Dan sat motionless for a moment or two. What was it Will Sperry had written him?

"Just wait until 'Zandeland twists its green fingers about your heart."

He breathed deeply. They had only touched down at Kisangani long enough to clear customs and change planes an hour or so before and had seen nothing of the Democratic Republic of the Congo, but Dan's pulse quickened, and he caught himself glancing at his watch again.

He turned to his younger brother, Ron, who was sitting beside him.

"Is it what you expected, Ron?" he asked.

"Not at all," Ron answered. "I thought it would be more–more–" He paused a while before continuing. "To tell you the truth, Danny, I don't know what I expected."

"I know exactly what you mean. I feel the same way."

The flight attendant, a slender, dark-skinned African, moved down the aisle and stopped beside them.

"A cup of coffee, monsieur?" he asked Ron in flawless French.

The boy looked at him quizzically.

"*Oui*," Dan broke in.

Ron turned to his brother.

"What was that all about?"

"He just asked if you wanted a cup of coffee, and I told him you did."

"How did you know I wanted coffee?" Ron asked.

"Don't you?"

"Sure, but I'd just like the chance of turning it down in case I didn't want any."

"Okay," Dan said laughing. "Next time I'll ask you first. Or I can just let you take care of everything."

"Oh, no!" Ron broke in quickly. "Don't do that or I'll starve to death."

The attendant brought coffee and two small cookies. For several minutes the boys were silent.

"When do we get to Isiro?" Ron asked.

Dan checked the time once more.

"We ought to be there in an hour."

Ron leaned back and closed his eyes. Moments later Dan did the same. Although they had slept fitfully on the flight from Cairo to Kisangani the night before, exhaustion suddenly overwhelmed them.

Dan wondered idly about Kay. It was eight o'clock in the morning back home. She had probably had devotions and was doing the dishes. Then he drifted off to sleep.

A few short months before, neither Dan nor Ron Orlis had ever thought it possible that they would be going to the DRC. Dan had been hard at work with his newly established charter plane service, and Ron had been busy at Cedarton Bible Institute. Neither of them had given any thought to going anywhere until Philip Ordman unexpectedly knocked at Dan's door.

* * *

It had been a snowy, blustering Saturday morning and the Orlis twins were visiting Dan and Kay for the weekend. Roxie was in the kitchen with Kay, and Ron was trying to write an English theme while he waited for Dan to come back from the Pawhasset airfield when there was a brisk knock at the door.

"See who it is, will you, Ron?" Kay called from the kitchen. "I'm up to my elbows in pie dough."

"If it's going to be cherry pie," he replied, "I'll do anything."

Ron pushed aside his books and got to his feet.

Through the half-frosted glass in the front door he could see the man on the porch. Ron paused.

Somehow the fellow looked vaguely familiar. He was a tall, angular individual, with graying hair just visible below his dark hat. He was well dressed but not expensively so. And the way he stood, with his back hunched against the wind, revealed that he was a stranger to Minnesota's harsh winters.

While Ron stared he knocked again.

"Ron," his sister called, "it's cold out there. Answer the door."

"Keep your hat on," he mumbled. "I'm going." The man at the door recognized him.

"Why, hello, Ron," he said genially. "I didn't expect to see you here."

"I–I should know you," the boy said uncertainly.

"You might not remember me, but I think you would remember my daughter, Wendy."

"Mr. Ordman!" Ron exclaimed. "I didn't expect to see you here."

"And I didn't expect to see you," Philip Ordman replied. "I thought you would be down at Cedarton Bible Institute."

He took off his boots and stepped into the small, simply furnished living room.

"Roxie and I came up for the weekend," Ron explained.

Kay and his sister came into the living room and talked with their guest for a moment or two.

"I'll call the airfield," Kay said, "and have Dan come home. I don't think he's doing anything that can't be put off until Monday."

Mr. Ordman glanced at his watch and got hurriedly to his feet.

"I didn't realize it was so late," he said. "Tell Dan I'll be back about 2 o'clock."

"Won't you stay for lunch?" Kay asked.

He hesitated.

"You won't get cherry pie like Kay's at the cafe," Ron told him.

It was not until after Dan came home and they had finished eating that the contractor revealed the purpose of his visit.

"I've often wondered how things have been going for you, Phil, since you left Guatemala," Dan said.

"I've been giving more and more of my time to mission building," the man answered, "and I've never been happier in my life."

There was a short silence.

Mr. Ordman took an overseas airmail letter from his pocket and held it thoughtfully.

"This letter is from the superintendent I sent down to the DRC to do some building for one of the big mission boards," he began. "Things haven't been going so well."

Dan leaned forward.

"What seems to be the trouble?"

Phil Ordman handed him the letter.

"There has been one work stoppage after another since we started building down there," the contractor continued. "Now Joe Mitchell, who has been superintendent there, has a virulent type of malaria that may make it necessary for him to come home."

"That is too bad," Dan said. He read the letter hurriedly. "Isn't there someone else who could take over and finish the building?"

Phil shook his head.

"No one who can be spared from the work," he said. "The missionaries are short-handed as it is." He replaced the letter in his pocket. "And what's worse, I don't have anyone qualified to send out and complete the job."

Dan's forehead wrinkled.

"You surely ought to be able to find someone to do it," he answered. "The building out there isn't too difficult, is it?"

"No," Mr. Ordman acknowledged, "the building in the DRC isn't too difficult. The construction and problems are very similar to those we faced in Guatemala."

"There was nothing out of the ordinary about those buildings," Dan said. "Anyone who has handled men ought to be able to put up the buildings without difficulty."

"That's right about the buildings," the contractor told him, "if they were to be put up here, but erecting them out there is another matter."

He leaned forward intently.

"Here a superintendent can order the things he needs. In the DRC the chances are he'll have to make a good many of them. He would have to make his own windows, doors and door frames, bricks, and so on. And in addition, he would have to be able to handle African workmen, some of whom know very little about modern construction."

"I see what you mean," Dan replied. "It would be difficult to find someone who could take care of things properly."

"That," the contractor concluded, "is why I have come to you."

"To me?" Dan echoed incredulously.

"I saw how you handled the nationals in Guatemala," Mr. Ordman went on. "I know you'd have the patience and the tact to work with Africans. And I saw plenty of improvising you had done."

"We had to improvise," Dan said, smiling. "There was nothing else to do."

"Exactly," Phil Ordman told him. "That's why it has to be done in Africa too." He paused for a moment.

"Would you and Ron be able to go down and take over the project in case Joe does have to come home?"

Dan took a long while to answer.

"I don't know," he said uncertainly. "Kay and I would have to talk it over. We'd want to pray about it."

"I didn't really expect an answer today," the contractor said. "But I thought it best to come up and talk with you so you could be considering it."

They spent an hour or more going over the project carefully. Dan and Ron learned that the building was to be done in East Congo on a station superintended by Will Sperry and his wife, Jean.

"They're veteran missionaries," Mr. Ordman explained, "with more than thirty years at Kindru."

"I think I've heard of them," Dan said.

"I'm not surprised," Mr. Ordman said. "I've never actually met Mr. Sperry, but I've heard about him for years."

"It sounds interesting," Dan said.

"Is there any big game hunting there?" Ron broke in.

"If we go, Ron," his brother said, "we'll be going to build, not to hunt."

"As a matter of fact," the contractor added, "there is a great deal of hunting there. And from what I've been able to learn, Will Sperry is able to use his hunting to give him contacts with the Africans."

"I read an article once about a missionary who did that," Ron said. "He'd make friends with the Africans by providing meat. Then he'd talk with them about Christ."

"That's just what Sperry does," Mr. Ordman said. "Then, too, he uses his rifle to provide meat for his work crew. Before Joe went out, Sperry wrote and asked him to bring along a rifle and apply for a license."

Ron's eyes brightened.

"I've already got my mind made up," he said.

That night Dan and Kay talked a long while about the offer to go to Africa.

"It will be hard for you here at home," Dan reminded her. "We're just getting our charter plane business started."

"We have a little savings," she reminded him. "The important thing is whether or not it's God's will."

By the time Mr. Ordman called two weeks later to tell them it was definite that the superintendent had to return home, they had their minds made up.

"We'll go," Dan said without hesitation.

CHAPTER 2

ON FOREIGN SOIL

The next few weeks were a frenzy of activity. There were shots to get, visas to apply for, plane reservations, and other plans to make. And in addition, Dan and Ron sent for a Lingala language book and studied furiously.

Kay had been the one who suggested it.

"Mr. Ordman thought we could get by with Danny's French," Ron told her. "He didn't think it would be necessary to learn an African language."

"You almost have to have a trade language," she said. "And from what I've been told it isn't particularly difficult."

"I can't even speak English," Ron grumbled. "How do you expect me to learn Lingala?"

"You won't be able to speak it fluently," she went on, "but you ought to be able to understand a little. You can at least have a start toward learning the language before you leave for Africa."

Although Ron had found Latin torture in high school, he was surprised at how quickly he was able to pick up Lingala. Both he and Dan had learned quite a bit of the African trade language by the time they were to leave for the Democratic Republic of Congo.

* * *

Now there was a small, sprawling community on the horizon. Ron poked his brother awake with his elbow.

"Danny," he said, "Danny, we're here!"

Dan awoke with a start.

The pilot banked the DC-3 and set it expertly on the end of the runway.

"I wonder if Mr. Sperry will be here to meet us?" Ron asked as the twin-engine craft rolled up before the small tropical air terminal.

"If he isn't, we're going to have a long walk. It's more than 200 miles up to Kindru."

"I like to walk," Ron said, "but not quite that far."

However, Will Sperry was at the terminal to meet them. The boys both spotted him before the plane came to a stop. He was a huge hulk of a man, with gray hair and a weather-beaten face that somehow reminded Dan of their dad. Two Africans, looking shorter than they actually were, stood behind the big missionary.

The missionary waved cheerily, and when they got off the plane, came forward to meet them.

He shook hands warmly.

"I'm sure glad to see you fellows," he said. "We've got a big job for you."

"Fine," Dan told him. "That's what we're here for."

While they waited for their luggage, Ron looked about. The jungle crowded in against the air strip on three sides, a lush, heavy growth that seemed almost impenetrable.

"It's the dry season," Mr. Sperry told him. "You ought to see it when everything is green."

They got their bags and went out to the pickup. Will Sperry must have been in town for several hours. The truck was loaded with bicycle tires, groceries, and gasoline drums. A battered bicycle was roped to the sideboards.

"Jean didn't come along," Mr. Sperry said. "So we'll only be three in the seat. We'll have lots of room."

"It wouldn't have bothered us to have four in here," Dan replied. "We can crowd up easily."

Mr. Sperry backed away from the air terminal and headed up the narrow, winding trail toward Kindru. It was shortly after noon and the direct rays of the sun were burning down on the little truck.

"When do you think we'll be able to start work?" Dan asked after a time.

"If the bricks are cool, we ought to get going right away," the missionary answered. "We'll check on that as soon as we get back."

They jounced through one small primitive village after another. Africans, hearing the sound of the motor, came running out to the road. When they saw who it was, they stood at attention or waved.

"Do all of these people know you?" Ron asked at last, "or do they act that way to everybody?"

Mr. Sperry chuckled.

"I guess they know me," he admitted.

The boys looked at him quizzically.

"Have you ever come over here to work?" Dan asked.

The missionary shook his head.

"Not exactly. But some of the people from here have been over at Kindru. I suppose I've fixed a bicycle or muzzle loader for someone in almost every one of those villages."

There was a short silence.

Ron expelled his breath slowly and Will Sperry glanced at him, a question in his eyes.

"What's the matter, Ron?" he asked.

"I–I probably shouldn't say it," the boy said, "but I couldn't help wondering how you'd have time to fix bicycles. Mr. Ordman said you are so awfully busy."

"That's one of the things we're busy doing," the missionary explained. "Back home a bicycle is just something that's nice to have. Out here a bicycle is almost a necessity for anyone who travels any distance at all. If an African doesn't have a bicycle in good working order, he has to walk."

"I see," Ron replied.

"But, of course, that's not the real reason we take time to repair bicycles," Mr. Sperry went on.

"Repairing bikes and muzzle loaders gives us a good contact with pagan Africans." He paused momentarily. "I couldn't tell you the number of men we've been privileged to lead to Christ while they waited for us to fix their bikes."

It was after dark when they finally pulled into the mission station on Kindru hill.

The following morning, Dan and Ron awakened sleepily to the sound of voices outside their bedroom window.

"Danny," Ron exclaimed, shaking his brother by the shoulder, "wake up! It must be the middle of the morning!"

Dan sat straight up in bed.

"What's that?" he demanded. "What's wrong?"

"I don't know," Ron told him, scrambling out of bed and making for the window, "but it sounds as though there's an army out here."

For a moment or two he stared at the scene below him.

"What is it?" Dan asked again.

"It's just a bunch of kids doing exercises," Ron said. He glanced at his watch. "What time have you got? My watch battery must be dying. It only says 6:30."

"That's what mine says too."

"That can't be right," Ron continued. "Nobody gets up this early to exercise."

They dressed quickly and went downstairs. Will Sperry was already in his office and his wife, Jean, was in the kitchen talking with the cook.

"That's just the school kids," she explained. "They start a little earlier on Saturday morning so they can finish school earlier."

When they had devotions and had finished breakfast, Mr. Sperry pushed back his chair and got to his feet.

"I sent a fellow up to check the brick kiln when we first got up this morning," he said. "I see he's back now."

Dan and Ron excused themselves and followed him out on the porch where the African was waiting for him.

They talked for a moment or two. As they did so, Will's lean face darkened.

He turned to the boys.

"It doesn't sound so good," he said. "He tells me he started to move the dirt, but it was still so hot he couldn't even get down to the bricks."

Dan moistened his lips.

"That means we'll have to wait, doesn't it?" Mr. Sperry nodded.

"We'll have to wait at least another week," he said, "and possibly two."

"I can't understand it," he continued. "We fired those bricks in plenty of time to have had them cool, and with a few days to spare."

"What would cause that?" Ron asked.

The missionary shrugged his shoulders.

"Who knows?" Then he smiled. "That's happened before, and I suppose it will happen again. An expert might know why, but I don't."

"That's sure too bad," Ron observed, unable to hide his disappointment. "I thought we'd be able to start work right away."

"That's one thing you soon learn here in Africa. Never to get in a hurry when things don't work out the way you think they should."

Dan said nothing for several minutes.

"There ought to be something we can do while we're waiting," he remarked at last. "What about the woodwork? Has all of that been made?"

"We cut down the trees months ago and have the logs seasoning, but we haven't started sawing them yet."

"Maybe we won't lose any time after all," Dan continued. "We could take a crew up to the village where the hospital is to be built and get the planks sawed out and planed and start making the window and door casings. Maybe we can have that work done by the time the bricks are cool enough to start laying them."

"Now that," Mr. Sperry said approvingly, "is the sort of talk I like to hear. You and I are going to get along."

Dan grinned.

"I guess I have to give credit to Dad for that," he said. "When something came up to stop him on one job back at the Angle, he always looked around to see what else he could do while he was waiting."

Sunday morning was spent visiting services on the hill and over at the leper colony, services that were conducted by earnest young African pastors.

In the evening, Will and Jean Sperry and the Orlises got together in the living room of the Sperry home for a time of Bible study and prayer. And the next morning they were all up before dawn, scurrying to get the truck loaded.

"There," Mr. Sperry said as the last piece of equipment was hoisted to the rear of the pickup, "I guess we're ready to go."

"How far is it to the place where we'll be building the dispensary and hospital?" Dan asked.

"About fifty miles. We're going up to the African village of Donguba."

Although it was still early in the morning when they left Kindru, Azande men and women and children already lined the road, walking or riding bicycles. When they saw the truck they moved quickly to the side of the narrow, twisting trail and melted back into the elephant grass or stood at attention, waving to the missionary and his wife as they went by.

"Why are you building the hospital at an out-of-the-way place like Donguba?" Ron asked. "Wouldn't it have been just as well to make the Kindru hospital a little bigger?"

Mr. Sperry shook his head.

"We are so far from the people up here that we haven't been able to reach them effectively. We are praying that the hospital will be a means of bringing some of them to Christ."

Ron thought about that.

"I figured almost everyone out here would have had a chance to hear the gospel," he said after a time, "with all the missionaries who are here."

Mr. Sperry shook his head.

"Far from it," he said. "And those who do hear – even those who become Christians – need someone to work with them for years to help them understand the gospel and what it means to live the Christian life."

He breathed deeply.

"If we had the money and the dedicated people, we could find places for twice as many missionaries as we have and still need more."

They had been driving an hour or more in the truck when they came upon a small group of children walking single file along the side of the road. They looked to be eight or ten years old. Each had a little bundle of clothes tied securely and balanced on top of his head.

"We haven't passed any houses for quite a while," Dan said. "Where did these children come from? And where are they going?"

"It looks as though they're moving," Ron put in.

"You're partly right about that," Jean Sperry told him. "Those children are going up to school."

Ron's eyes widened.

"But didn't you say there aren't any schools or hospitals up here for miles and miles?"

"That's right," she answered. "Those youngsters are walking up the road to school. And it's more than eighty miles."

Ron whistled in amazement.

"It will take them three days if they have to walk all the way," she said. "They'll stay for three months and then walk home to stay for one month."

"And the kids at home think it's terrible if they have to walk a mile," Dan commented.

Mr. Sperry stopped the truck and the youngsters scrambled up on the load of supplies and tools.

"We'll save them a day's walking," the missionary said.

It was almost noon when they reached the village where the hospital and dispensary were to be built. As soon as they stopped, the Africans began to help unload the truck.

"Hey, this is service!" Ron said.

"Most of them are so glad to see the missionary they'll do most anything for us," Mrs. Sperry explained.

Dan and Ron would have helped, but a white boy about Ron's age came up just then and Will Sperry introduced him to them.

"This is Sid Rucker," he said. "His parents have a small store up the road a way."

The newcomer allowed a faint smile to alight briefly on his lips.

"Come on over and sit down," he said, indicating a log that had been pulled up near the ashes of a dead campfire. "The Africans will unload that truck. It's all they've got to do."

Ron watched the men work for a moment or two.

"There doesn't seem to be room to get around the truck," he said.

"They'll work," Sid replied.

There was a note of incredulity in his voice.

"We have a beastly time getting them to do anything for us, but they'll work for Will Sperry. They'll do anything he wants them to do, and half the time they'll work for nothing."

"That's because they love him," Ron answered.

Sid Rucker snorted and ran his hand through his heavy black hair.

"I don't get it," he said. "I don't get it at all."

CHAPTER 3

NATIVES AT WORK

Will and Jean Sperry spent the day in the little African village of Donguba, helping Dan and Ron get settled in the rest house the Africans had built for the missionaries when they visited in the area.

"There!" Will said when the last mosquito netting had been hung over the beds. "You ought to be comfortable here."

"Don't worry about us," Dan assured him. "We'll get along all right."

"I'm sure you will," the missionary said. "I'd like to stay for a day or two and help get the work started, but we have so many things to take care of back at Kindru that we just can't stay any longer."

Mr. and Mrs. Sperry got into the truck.

"Just tell the guys what you want them to do," he said again, "and supervise a little so you're sure they understand what you want. With your French and the little Lingala you've picked up you ought to get along fine."

"When do you think you'll be back?" Ron asked.

"That's something we never know," Will answered. "We hope to make it in a week or so. It depends entirely on how long it takes us to go down to Isiro and back. We've got to get some glass and hardware and a few things we don't have at Kindru."

The boys stood at the corner of the rest house and watched while the Sperrys drove out of sight.

"Now," Dan said, "to get to work."

"We won't start work until morning, will we, Danny?" Ron asked.

Dan laughed.

"The Sperrys are only a mile down the road. Don't tell me you want to start goofing off already."

"You know better than that," Ron answered defensively, "but it's going to be dark in half an hour."

"Okay," Dan told him. "Since you insist, we'll wait to start work in the morning. But I do want to take a look at those mahogany logs Will Sperry has seasoning. We're going to have to work out some way of holding them so we can saw them into planks."

He called Ebele, the African pastor, to take them to the place where the logs were piled.

"This way," Ebele said in Lingala.

They were leaving the village when two stalwart young Africans stepped out of the elephant grass ahead of them.

Ebele stopped and spoke to them in 'Zande.

For an instant or two they stared at Dan and Ron.

They were handsome, powerfully built young men, barefooted and dressed in tattered shorts.

The setting sun glistened on their ebony shoulders and the blades of their razor-sharp spears.

Danny smiled and took half a step forward.

"*Mbote* (Greetings)," they said, shaking hands gravely.

"These are Ngida and Deseli," Ebele said, "the sons of the chief."

"We hope to see you in the services while we're working here," Dan told them.

Their smiles faded momentarily.

"Maybe," Ngida said without enthusiasm.

They stepped aside and allowed the Orlises and the pastor to continue down the path.

"They didn't act too friendly," Danny said at last.

"They are friendly enough," Ebele answered. "It is just that they have no time for the things of Christ. The pull of pagan ways is strong in them."

"I suppose Will Sperry has tried to talk to them," Ron said.

"*Oui*," Ebele replied, "and so have Dr. Roy Kleinschmidt and his wife when they come up to hold a clinic. Sometimes Deseli and Ngida listen. Sometimes no."

The following morning, Dan and Ron took a crew of men out to the pile of mahogany logs. Mr. Sperry had anticipated the problem of sawing them and had piled them on a steep side hill where they could easily be rolled out on sawhorses, one at a time.

The Africans took the big saw and started to work rhythmically, one standing on the log and the other below it. The red sawdust filtered down into a little cone.

The time passed swiftly and it was noon before either Dan or Ron realized it.

"This is really going all right," Ron said. "If we can keep them going at this rate, we'll have the woodwork and windows finished before we know it."

"It's a good thing," Dan said. "There are a lot of things to do."

When they got back to the rest house, Sidney Rucker was waiting for them.

"Hi," he said, waving to them from the chair where he was sprawling. "Thought I'd come over and see how you're getting along this morning."

"Couldn't be better," Dan replied. "Are you looking for a job?"

"Not me," Sid countered. "I'm allergic to work. I just came over to see if you'd like to go hunting this afternoon. This is a great place to hunt."

"We'd sure like to," Dan said, "and we hope to get in some hunting before we go back. But right now we've got a lot of work to do."

The scrawny boy got to his feet.

"I sure can't figure you guys out," he said. "You come way out here just to build a hospital for a bunch of ignorant savages who won't appreciate it."

"We're not building the hospital so they'll appreciate it," Dan explained. "We're building it to help them and to give our medical missionaries a chance to preach Christ to them when they come in for treatment."

They went into the rest house and sat down.

"Why don't you people leave the natives with their pagan religion?" Sid persisted. "They're happy."

Dan looked at him.

"Are they?" he asked. "Are they happy fearing evil spirits? Are they happy in their superstition and ignorance?"

Sid grinned sheepishly.

"I suppose there are times when they aren't very happy," he admitted grudgingly, "but they don't work, and they sure have a lot of fun."

"Have you ever talked with a mature Christian African about that?" Dan continued. "Have you ever asked someone like Ebele whether he was happier as a pagan than he's been as a Christian?"

The boy shook his head.

"Do it some time. You'll find out that the only true happiness a person such as Ebele has ever known has been since he became a believer."

Sid fell silent.

"Have you ever considered the claims of Christ on your life?" Dan asked.

The boy's body stiffened.

"I came to see if you want to go hunting," he answered curtly. "If you don't, I'll be on my way."

He pushed his chair back from the table and stood.

"We'll go hunting with you," Dan said, "but we've got to get our work rolling before we can think about that."

"Is there really good hunting around here?" Ron asked.

"The best," Sid answered. As the subject changed, he relaxed a little. "You can get 'most anything you want here and without working too hard either. Baboons, wild pigs, buffalo, waterbuck, wildebeest. You can even shoot an elephant if you want to."

Ron stared at him.

"An elephant!" he echoed. "Are you kidding?"

"If you'll go hunting with me, I'll show you whether I'm kidding or not. This whole area is alive with elephants and all sorts of game. But then you guys probably wouldn't have backbone enough to go after it."

During the next few days the men worked diligently. As soon as the men had sawed several planks, Dan put others to planing and scraping. He and Ron went from one group to the other, checking their work and showing them how to do it a little better.

"You know," Ron said one evening, "I always thought it would be hard to teach the people to do good work of any kind, but it's not. These people catch on fast."

"Of course they do," Dan answered. "Most of them don't have any education and they're steeped in superstitions and pagan ways, but they are intelligent and can learn."

From time to time one or another of the Africans came to Dan.

"There are buffaloes in the waterhole, just outside the village," they would say. Or, "We just saw six waterbucks in that burned-over grass." Or, "There is elephant sign up the road half a mile."

Dan's answer was always the same.

"I wish we could do something about it, but we don't have time for that now."

The light went out of their eyes, but they did not protest.

On one occasion, Sid was loafing nearby when one of the workers approached Dan.

"What's the matter?" he asked when the African had returned to work. "Haven't you got your courage yet?"

"What do you mean?" Dan asked.

"Skip it," the boy said. "You'll keep on giving one excuse after another for not going hunting until it's time for you to go back to America."

They were still talking when a little cloud of dust was observed to the south. It moved closer along the road and was accompanied by the crescendoing hum of a motor.

"Sounds as though someone is coming," Dan said.

"In a tank," Ron added.

At that moment a white truck lurched into view and squealed to a stop before the rest house.

"It's the Doc," Sid said.

A tall, lanky white-haired man got out of the driver's seat and approached them.

"You must be the Orlises," he began. "I'm Roy Kleinschmidt and this is my wife, Coralee."

Dan and Ron shook hands with them.

"We stayed with Will and Jean last night," Dr. Roy continued, "and they told us about you. We're certainly glad to have you. We need this hospital badly."

"Could you hear us coming?" Mrs. Kleinschmidt broke in. "We hit a rock and knocked the muffler off a few miles down the road."

"To tell you the truth," Ron answered, "when we heard it, we thought it was a tank."

The doctor and his wife both laughed.

The Africans had opened the back of the truck and began to set up the doctor's equipment under a crude grass-covered shade built for the purpose.

"We didn't expect to be here so soon," Dr. Roy said to Dan and Ron, "but I've been asked to take over a hospital up the road 150 kilometers or so. We're to be there for a couple of months."

"So," his wife broke in, "we decided to come up a few days early and hold our clinic here."

She was an efficient woman with a quick smile and a radiance all her own.

She went into the rest house, changed into her white uniform, and set to work.

While the doctor examined the more serious cases, she treated ulcers and talked with the women about the importance of regularly removing chiggers from the feet of their children.

"We can take them out for you," she said, "but we don't come around often enough to do it. You must take care of them yourselves."

Ron moved up beside her.

"Did chiggers cause his feet to be like that?" he asked, looking down at a boy's scabbed feet.

"Not the kind of chiggers we have at home," she answered. "These lay eggs in the skin and grow to about the size of a pea. They can spread in a child's foot if they aren't taken out right away. Often they cause infection and sometimes the toes come off."

Ron watched while the boy's mother cut away the callouses on the bottom of his foot with a razor blade and used a pointed stick to remove the chiggers. He winced with pain but did not cry out.

Dr. Kleinschmidt worked methodically, checking one patient after another. As he made his examinations, he spoke with each one about the Lord Jesus. He seemed to know each African by name and whether or not he was a Christian. If he was pagan, the doctor spoke of salvation. If he professed to be a Christian, he talked of the Christian life and what is expected of a believer.

As time passed and word that the doctor had arrived spread among the people who lived in nearby villages, the line of patients grew. At last the doctor looked at his watch and stopped.

"We'll see the rest of you tomorrow," he told them. "And don't forget the service here tonight. We hope you'll all be out for it."

Several Africans thanked him profusely for help he had given them or their families in the past. He had time for each one, speaking very gently to them.

"It must be fascinating to work with these people," Ron said later as he helped the doctor pack his equipment and drugs.

"It is," Dr. Roy answered. "But, of course, the most wonderful thing is to lead one of them to Christ and then take him on in his faith until he begins to shed his old pagan practices."

Dan and Ron wanted to vacate the rest house for the Kleinschmidts, but they would not hear of it.

"We've got our truck equipped to sleep in," Coralee said. "It would be nice if we could eat with you, or you with us, but we'd much prefer to sleep in our truck."

"That sounds all right to us," Dan said, "if you're sure it's all right with you. But we can easily move out of the rest house."

"I don't care where we sleep," Dr. Roy said, "as long as I can crawl into bed right after dinner. It looks as though I have more patients here now than I'll be able to take care of, and we'll have to leave the day after tomorrow."

"If you could see the more serious patients here, Roy," his wife suggested, "I could stay on and take care of the others."

"That might be the solution at that," the doctor replied thoughtfully. "You could take care of a good many just as well as I, and there are nurses up at

Watsi. We'll be short-handed, but we could get by for a few days."

He smiled and put his arm about her.

"We'll see how it goes tomorrow."

Sid, who had been standing quietly by all afternoon, shook his head.

"It doesn't make sense to me," he said, "spending all this time and effort on a bunch of ignorant Africans."

Before any of them could reply, Ngida and Deseli came bursting out of the grass and dashed up to them. Perspiration glistened on their dark bodies and their breath was coming in thin, tearing gasps.

"What's the matter?" Dan cried.

"An elephant!" Ngida almost shouted. "He was in our garden!"

He spoke so excitedly the words came tumbling out, an almost unintelligible mixture of 'Zande, French, and Lingala.

"What?" Dan repeated.

"There was an elephant in our garden!" Ngida said again.

"And when we tried to drive him away," Deseli broke in, "he charged us!"

Dan turned to Dr. Roy.

"What does that mean?" he asked. "Is it serious?"

The doctor nodded.

"The people depend on their gardens for food. And there's nothing more destructive than an elephant."

Dan's face furrowed.

"Do you hunt, Dr. Roy?" he asked.

The doctor shook his head. "I've never fired a gun in my life," he said.

Sid laughed mirthlessly.

"Now you are in a spot, Orlis," he said. "Let's see you get out of this one!"

CHAPTER 4

TRACKING AN ELEPHANT

Ngida looked at Dan appealingly.

"You will go with us?" he asked. "You will help us get the garden elephant?"

Dan nodded and turned to his brother.

"Go, get the guns!" he said crisply.

"Do you mean it?" Ron asked tensely.

"You don't have to show off before us, Orlis," Sid said scornfully. "You're among friends. You don't have to show what a big, brave hero you are."

While Ron was in the rest house getting the high-powered rifles, Dr. and Mrs. Kleinschmidt called Dan to one side.

"Dan," Dr. Roy said softly, "have you ever been elephant hunting?"

"No, but I've done a lot of hunting up on the Angle back in the States. Dad used to run a hunting lodge every fall, and I helped when I was home."

"This isn't like hunting back in the States," the doctor went on. "Elephant hunting is dangerous. They're smart, unpredictable, and hard to kill."

"I'll be careful," Dan promised.

"And, Dan," he continued, "don't depend on the Africans if the going gets rough."

"What do you mean?"

"They'll go off and leave you," Dr. Roy said. "All they've ever hunted with has been old muzzle-loading rifles and spears. And the only defense they've ever had against an animal like an elephant has been to run and get out of his way. I've only heard of one African who could be depended on in a tough situation." He breathed deeply. "And he doesn't live here."

"Thanks for the warning," Dan said. "I'll keep my eyes open."

"We'll pray for you, Dan," Coralee murmured as Ron returned.

Dan took one Winchester and threw back the bolt.

"Did you bring any cartridges?" he asked.

"A whole box," Ron answered. "You wanted steel jackets, didn't you?"

Dan nodded.

"We'd better take a few lead bullets along, but we'll use these if we get a shot at that elephant."

He filled the magazine of one rifle, flicked on the safety, and checked it, holding the barrel in the air. Deseli, who was standing beside him, took the gun so Danny could load the other one.

"I think I'm going along," Sid announced boisterously. "This is something I've got to see."

Coralee glanced up at the sun that seemed to be riding on the treetops in the west.

"It might be best not to follow the elephant into the jungle," she said, "at least not after dark. It's the most treacherous animal out here."

Ngida turned to Dan impatiently.

"We ready now?" he asked.

Dan nodded, and the young African struck off across the road and into the elephant grass and scrub trees on the opposite side.

Ngida was proudly carrying his old muzzle-loader over his shoulder. Dan was followed by Deseli, who carried his rifle, and the second gun bearer was only a step behind Ron. Sid followed the gun bearer, and three spear-armed 'Zande hunters completed the party.

The little procession marched single file past some native huts, skirted a cotton field, crossed a little patch of *sabi* grass, and came to another garden.

Ngida stopped and waved his arm expressively.

"See!" he exclaimed. "Elephant!"

Dan gasped involuntarily.

He had known they would see destruction, but he was not prepared for the scene before them. The garden was a shambles. It looked as though a gigantic steam roller had run wild over the crooked rows. Papaya and mango trees had been snatched up by the roots and trampled underfoot. The manioc had been ground underfoot until the thin, willowlike bushes were almost pulverized. And the cotton had been trampled until the plants were scarcely recognizable.

Small wonder the Africans considered an elephant in the garden such a tragedy!

"I'd sure feel terrible if I were the one who had been taking care of this garden for the last few months," Ron whispered.

"Ngida didn't take care of this garden," Sid said. "His wife has been doing it. The women do all the work out here."

"Just the same, it would be a tough break."

Ngida moved cautiously across the garden, studying the huge tracks intently. Several minutes later he stopped suddenly. The others did the same.

"He's not far away, *bwana*," he whispered. "You better take this gun."

Dan did so.

His hands were trembling and wet with perspiration. He put the rifle to his shoulder and peered through the scope in the growing darkness. It was going to be difficult to aim carefully with so little light.

Ron turned to his gun bearer and took the second rifle.

"We go quietly," Ngida whispered in warning. "The elephant, he hear very good."

The chief's son seemed to glide silently over the parched stubble. They crossed a narrow stretch of burned-over grass and entered the forest.

"There's no doubt about which way the fellow went," Ron whispered as they passed a tree that had been ripped out by the roots and flung aside.

"He looks like a bad one," Sid said uneasily. "A guy can't be too careful when you're tracking an elephant. You can't tell what he's going to do." He breathed deeply. "And believe me, they can cause a lot of harm if they get riled up."

Ron's lithe body was trembling with excitement. He touched the rifle safety uneasily.

Ngida continued to inch forward. He studied each track with care, pausing at times to listen intently.

"How far do you usually have to follow an elephant before catching up with him?" Ron asked.

"That depends on a lot of things," Sid replied. "It's nothing to follow an elephant for a day or two if he's taken the notion to travel. He might go straight off into the jungle and scarcely stop to eat. Or he might not travel more than a hundred yards or so. Sometimes, if an elephant knows he's being followed, he'll double back and attack from the side or the rear."

Ron shivered.

"Every time I go along elephant hunting," Sid continued, "I wonder why I was foolish enough to do it."

"You keep that up," Ron told him, "and you'll have me running off before we even see an elephant."

The little group had been so intent on following the huge animal they scarcely noticed that the sun had gone down until suddenly it was dark.

Ngida stopped.

"We'd better turn back," he said, his voice betraying a new uneasiness. "It is dark and the elephant is headed for the waterhole."

"How far is it?" Dan asked him.

"Not far, *bwana,*" the African answered.

"I brought a powerful light along," Dan continued. "Let's go on and see if we can get a shot at him."

"No, *bwana,*" Ngida said, his voice rising. "We not go to the waterhole."

"But he might come back and get into somebody else's garden tonight if we don't get him," Dan protested. "And we've already followed him this far."

The African's body straightened.

"We not go there," he repeated firmly. "Not to the waterhole."

With that he turned with a finality that startled Dan and stalked back toward the village. There was nothing for the others to do but follow him.

Dan said no more to him until they returned to the village. Then he called Ngida off to one side.

"Maybe we get another chance at the elephant," the African said, "when he is not at the waterhole."

"What has that got to do with it?" Dan asked.

Ngida did not answer.

"Why did you stop us from going after him?"

"It was dark," Ngida replied evasively. "It is not safe to follow an elephant after dark."

The answer seemed logical enough, but there was something disturbing about Ngida's manner.

"If that is all it is," he went on, "we'll go out after the elephant first thing in the morning. If we get started at dawn, we ought to be able to get over to the waterhole and be back in a couple of hours."

He could not see Ngida's face in the darkness, but he heard the young African gasp.

"Oh, no, *bwana!*"

"No, *bwana!*" Deseli echoed, almost in chorus with his brother. "We cannot go to the waterhole."

"And why not?" Dan asked. "If that's where the elephant is, why can't we go there after him?"

"We can go to the waterhole," Ngida said, "but first we must offer sacrifices to the god of the waterhole. That is why we couldn't go there tonight and why we can't go in the morning."

"Sacrifices?" Dan repeated. "What do you mean?"

"It is not safe to go to the waterhole," Deseli broke in, "until sacrifices have been made to the god of the waterhole."

"No one dares to go there to hunt," Ngida explained, "unless he has first offered sacrifices to the god of the waterhole. And even if it wasn't dangerous, we wouldn't be able to kill anything unless the sacrifices have been made."

Dan sat down in a native chair and the Africans gathered about him in silence.

"The God of the Bible is the God of all the world," he began patiently in Lingala. "He is the God of the waterhole. The God of the jungle. The God of the grasslands. He made all the world and everything that is in it. All belongs to Him."

The Africans moved closer, their interest growing.

"Is He more powerful than the god of the waterhole?" Ngida asked.

"There are no other gods than Him," Dan repeated. "He has not only made us, He has provided us with a way to be saved. The only way a person can be saved."

Carefully, he explained the way of salvation; how they must confess their sin and put their trust in the Lord Jesus Christ.

"But, *bwana*," Deseli protested when he had finished, "what does that have to do with making a sacrifice to the waterhole god?"

Dan got his Bible and a kerosene lamp from the rest house and opened the Book. He could not read Lingala, but he opened his English Bible to the book of I Kings and translated as he went along.

". . . So they prepared two bulls to be put on the altar. One was taken by the priests of the god Baal (he was like the god of your waterhole) and Elijah, the servant of the living God, took the other. They piled wood under both altars but didn't build a fire. Then the priests of Baal called for him to set the wood afire. And do you know what happened?"

"There was none?" Ngida asked incredulously.

"That's exactly right. There was none. Then Elijah drenched the wood and the bull and the other altar with water. He prayed to the God of the Bible, the only God. Fire came down from heaven and burned the wood, the bull, and the altar."

He paused significantly.

The Africans looked from one to the other, silently.

"Which God is the real God?" Dan asked.

They thought about that for a moment or two.

"We go," Ngida said reluctantly. "We go with you to the waterhole. But it would be better if we offered the sacrifice."

Dan stared after him.

Dr. Kleinschmidt came up beside him.

"Don't feel so bad, Dan," he said. "We missionaries have been battling that sort of thing for many years. The roots of their old culture run deep. We have to keep hacking away at them, but the progress is slow."

Sid hung around until Dr. Roy went back into the rest house. Then he approached Dan.

"You'd have been a lot better off to have let them make their sacrifices," he said.

"But we couldn't do that," Dan protested. "That's pagan. It's the sort of thing the missionaries must stamp out if they are going to make Christians of these people and free them of their fears."

"Just you wait," Sid went on. "You'd have done a lot better to have let them sacrifice something. That would have put some courage in their backbones. The way it is now they'll lead you out there to that elephant and get so scared they'll run off and leave you! That's what'll happen!"

CHAPTER 5

"THAT'S THE ONE!"

Dan wanted to talk with Dr. Roy and his wife that night, but they were busy with the Africans until time for bed.

"I guess it doesn't really make any difference," he said, slipping off his shoes. "They probably couldn't help us anyway."

"I'd like to talk with them just the same," Ron said. "I've been thinking about what Sid said a little while ago. Do you suppose the Africans would actually run off and leave us if we got in a bad spot?"

"I wouldn't pay much attention to what Sid told us," Dan answered. "He's apt to say 'most anything to give us a bad time. But Dr. Roy said something that makes me think Sid was telling the truth."

Ron shivered.

"That's sure a pleasant thought," he said. "To think

that everyone is apt to run off and leave us if that elephant takes a notion to come our way."

"There's not much use in worrying about that now," Dan said. "We don't even know if we're going to get close enough to take a shot at him."

Ron crawled into bed.

"If I wasn't so anxious to go elephant hunting, I'd be in favor of giving it up," he said.

"You can stay here and keep the guys on the job if you want to," Dan told him.

"Oh, no, you don't!" the boy countered. "You're not going to get rid of me that easily."

He closed his eyes to dream of elephants taking after him from every direction and natives scrambling through the brush. During one such dream, a huge one-tusked elephant they were stalking turned on them. He threw up his head, his trunk writhing like a thing alive as it tested the air. Great ears fanned outward and quivered tensely.

Ron felt the strength go out of his body, leaving him limp and helpless.

Then, without warning, the elephant trumpeted his anger and charged wildly toward the terror-stricken hunter. Ron reached back for his rifle.

"My gun," he whispered between clenched teeth.

He expected the gun bearer to thrust the weapon into his hands, but he did not. He glanced around. Both gun bearer and gun were gone!

And the great beast was bearing down on him! One tree was bowled over and then another!

"My rifle!" Ron shouted aloud in the stillness of the night. "Give me my rifle!"

Instantly everyone was awake.

Dan grasped Ron by the shoulders.

"What's the matter?" he cried. "What's wrong, Ron?"

Africans came charging into the rest house, spears ready, and the Kleinschmidts scrambled out of their truck.

"What's going on in here?" Mrs. Kleinschmidt demanded, shining her flashlight about the small room.

Ron was sitting up in bed, shaking his head.

"Who killed him?" he asked. "Who killed him?"

"Who killed whom?" she asked. "What are you talking about?"

"That elephant that was about to get me," Ron repeated. "Who killed him?"

"You were just dreaming," Dan said.

By this time Ron was fully awake. He grinned sheepishly.

"I–I'm sorry," he mumbled.

"I should think you would be," the doctor's wife said, masking the smile on her face. "You should have stayed asleep and found out what it's like to be chased by an elephant."

"I know that already," Ron told her. "Believe me!"

It seemed to Ron that morning was long in coming. But at last Dr. and Mrs. Kleinschmidt began to stir around the improvised kitchen on the veranda of the rest house. Ron and Dan got up and joined them in the early morning darkness.

"Well," Coralee asked when she saw Ron, "did the elephant come after you again?"

"I didn't give him a chance," Ron answered. "I decided I'd better steer clear of elephants."

Mrs. Kleinschmidt hurried with breakfast and the boys were just finishing when Ngida and Deseli came up. They stood respectfully at some distance from the rest house until Ron and Dan left the table. Then they approached.

"Is everything ready, Ngida?" Dan asked.

"*Oui,*" the African replied. There was a note of hostility in his voice. "But we are not so sure about going after the elephant this morning. The god of the waterhole will be very angry."

"Maybe he even hurt somebody," Deseli added.

"We went over all of that last night," Dan told them patiently. "It's as I said. There is nothing to worry about on this hunt more than any other. There is no god of the waterhole."

In the growing light Dan could see the disbelief on their faces.

"I hope you are right, *bwana,*" Ngida said doubtfully.

By this time all of the Africans who were going on the elephant hunt had gathered at the village.

They were just ready to leave when Sid came riding up on his bicycle.

"You didn't think you were going to get away without me, now did you, Danny?" the boy demanded. "You sure wouldn't make me miss out on all the fun."

"We're glad to have you along," Dan told him.

"After my dream last night," Ron said, "the more guns we take, the better I'll like it. I can still see that old boy bearing down on me."

Sid laughed.

"I'd like to take my gun along to rescue you," he said, "but I haven't got my license yet. And you wouldn't want anyone to hunt without a license. Not good Christians like you."

Dan told Ngida they were ready to leave, and the lithe young African led them. Ngida moved forward but with obvious reluctance. His spear quivered slightly in his hand and his breathing was noisy and labored. Deseli was even more disturbed. He hung back until Dan almost stepped on his heels.

"What's the matter up there?" Ron whispered.

Dan turned and shook his head.

"What did I tell you?" Sid said. "They're so scared now they're about ready to go skedaddling off into the woods." He laughed shortly. "If someone jumped out from behind a tree and said 'boo,' we'd be left here all by our lonesome."

Ngida stopped and looked back.

Sid spoke to him in 'Zande.

The African started and his face grew taut.

"What's the matter?" Dan asked in Lingala.

Deseli looked at his brother appealingly.

"What's wrong?"

"*Bwana,*" Ngida answered at last, his voice

quavering, "it is not good for us to go on. The god of the waterhole will be so angry he will destroy us all if we do not make the sacrifice."

Dan whirled to face the boy who had accompanied them.

"What did you say to him, Sid?" he demanded.

The boy sneered. "I only asked him what time it was," he said tauntingly. "There's no law against that, is there?"

"If you speak to any of the Africans in 'Zande again or talk so low we can't hear what you're saying, you'll have to go back." Dan's voice was firm, and there was no mistaking his determination, but he spoke without raising his voice.

Sid recoiled involuntarily.

"You don't need to get so huffy about it," he protested. "I was just having a little fun."

"I'm not huffy," Dan repeated in the same firm, even tone, "but I don't think anyone could say he was having fun by scaring someone who is already frightened. And I don't intend to stand for any more of it. You're welcome to go with us, but only if you stop interfering."

"Okay, okay," Sid retorted. "If that's the way you feel about it, I won't say anything 'more to them. But just remember what I told you. They'll run out on you just when you need them the most."

Dan turned to Ngida and talked with him and his brother. He went over the story of Elijah and the priests of Baal once more, explained the way of salvation, and quoted verses to show that God is the only living God.

"If you say it is all right, *bwana*," Ngida went on, "we go on."

"I am not lying to you," Dan said.

"We go." The African spoke with a firmness that had not been present in his voice before.

Deseli grasped him by the arm.

"No!" he said tensely. "No!"

"We go," his brother repeated.

Ngida picked up his spear, turned, and marched down the trail purposefully. Deseli followed him.

Dan looked about, almost fearfully. What would the Africans do if the elephant charged?

Ron put the question into words, whispering softly in his ear.

"Maybe the elephant won't even be in the waterhole."

"I–I'm not so sure I want to find him," Ron replied.

By that time Ngida had picked up the fresh tracks of the huge beast and began to follow them with great care through the tall grass.

"The tracks are fresh," the African whispered almost in Dan's ear, "less than an hour old."

Dan and Ron pushed forward to examine a huge track that must have been all of twenty inches in diameter. Ngida hunched over it intently.

"He was going this way," he explained, "very slowly." He straightened and his words were haunted with fear. "He is at the waterhole."

"He headed that way, all right," Ron agreed, "but that sure doesn't mean he stopped there. He probably got a drink, wallowed in the water, and kept right on going through the grass or jungle."

Ngida shook his head.

"Not him," he said prophetically. "He is at the waterhole."

"If he's there," Dan said crisply, more to get the subject on safer ground, "we'd better get on the move. There's no telling when he'll take a notion to leave."

"*Oui*," Ngida answered.

He continued down the trail and Deseli followed him. Dan, sensing their growing fear, pressed close behind to keep them moving.

Five minutes passed, and then ten.

Suddenly the African tracker stopped and held a hand in the air.

"The elephant is up there," Ngida hissed.

Only Deseli and Dan heard the words, but the others knew the meaning of the upraised hand. Excitement rippled up the trail.

Dan reached back, and the gun bearer shoved the big rifle into his outstretched hand. Mechanically, he checked the magazine and, his hand on the safety, began to creep forward.

Ngida and Deseli moved into the elephant grass on each side of the trail to permit Dan to pass.

He caught his breath sharply as he drew up even with the tracker.

The huge animal stood there peacefully, feeding on the leaves of a tree he had uprooted a few moments before. His great ears lay motionless against his shoulders as he moved a few feet to reach the more tender leaves. Muscles rippled smoothly beneath the slate-gray skin as he walked.

A few minutes passed and Dan stared at the elephant that was feeding some 25 or 30 yards away. The big animal turned, and the boy's breath caught in his throat. For the first time he caught sight of the great, curving tusks. They were so big and cumbersome the elephant seemed to lift them ponderously.

Dan was so fascinated by what he saw that the gun lay forgotten in his hands.

"*Bwana,*" Ngida whispered in his ear at last, "that is the one!"

Dan started. The sound of the tense voice brought him back to reality.

"Are you sure?" he whispered. "Is that the elephant that has been in your garden?"

"*Oui, bwana,*" the African said. "That's the one! I'd know him anywhere!"

Crouching behind a clump of scrub brush, Dan crept forward, raising the gun to his shoulder as he did so. The safety off, he found the elephant in the scope and set the crosshairs on a spot just below the elephant's ear.

The great beast seemed to sense the danger. He froze, motionless for an instant or two.

Carefully Dan squeezed the trigger.

The roar of the high-powered rifle reverberated through the still morning air. The elephant's head snapped up and he whirled to stare at them. His trunk went high, testing the air! His huge ears stood straight out from his body, straining to catch any sound.

"You missed him!" Ron whispered.

Without taking the rifle from his shoulder, Dan ejected the empty cartridge and squeezed the trigger a second time. As the gun went off the elephant charged wildly into the jungle.

The sound of the rifle shattered the silence a second time and reverberated across the hills. Then all was quiet once more. Dan stared at the rifle in disbelief.

"I missed him," he said incredulously. "At twenty-five yards I missed him!"

"It was the god of the waterhole," Ngida answered. "We did not sacrifice to him, so he spoiled your aim. He kept you from killing the elephant."

"*Oui,*" Deseli affirmed. "No one can kill anything here until he has first made a sacrifice to the god of the waterhole to keep him from getting angry." He paused and lowered his voice significantly. "It is a wonder he did not kill us all!"

"But that is ridiculous," Dan said, shaking his head. "There is no god of the waterhole."

"We have seen," Ngida told him. "And he is more powerful than your God or you would have killed the elephant. Never again do we come here without making the sacrifice."

Dan tried to talk with him, but he refused to listen.

"I suppose we might just as well go back."

They turned and retraced their steps back to the village. Even Sid remained silent.

Mrs. Kleinschmidt looked up as they came back to the rest house. She noted in a glance that something was wrong.

"What happened?"

Ron told her.

"That is too bad," she said. "Ngida and Deseli are so superstitious. Something like this will probably drive them even farther from the Lord."

"I still can't understand how Dan could miss an animal that big," Ron told her and her husband. "He's an excellent shot with either a rifle or a shotgun."

"I can't understand it, either," Dan said. "No one misses a shot that easy without a reason."

Ron took the steel-jacketed bullets from his rifle and went into the rest house with it. Sid, who had been watching from some distance away, moved closer.

"Maybe it's as Ngida and Deseli say," he ventured. "The god of the waterhole just wouldn't let you hit that elephant."

Dan looked up at him quizzically and called out to his brother.

"Bring your rifle and a couple of bullets, Ron. I want to check these guns."

"You never give up, do you, Orlis?" Sid demanded. "Why don't you just admit that the waterhole god outfoxed you and let it go at that? You aren't cut out to be a hunter anyway."

Dan and Ron went to a safe spot some distance from the village and set up a target about a hundred yards away. Sid followed them.

"What's this all about?" Ron asked curiously.

"He's just trying to find some way of saving face," Sid taunted.

For answer Dan aimed carefully, resting the rifle barrel in the crotch of a tree. The bullet crashed into the tree at least a yard above the target, almost splitting it in two.

"There's something wrong with that gun!" Ron cried. "Even I wouldn't miss a target so far at a hundred yards."

Dan's mouth tightened as he examined the rifle expertly.

"I don't know why I didn't think to examine the rifles before," he said. "Somebody has been tampering with this scope."

He pointed to the rear mount.

"The back of the scope has been raised to cause the gun to shoot high."

"Who would do a thing like that?" Ron wanted to know.

Dan turned to Sid. The boy started to laugh, but the gleam in Dan's eyes drove the laughter away.

"It was you," he said.

Sid cringed a little.

"That's about like you, Orlis," he blustered. "You

try to blame someone else for your own blunders. It's about like you."

Dan took a step toward him, and Sid backed away.

"You tampered with these guns," he repeated.

Sid's lips began to quiver.

"If you've got to have someone to blame your lousy shooting on, I suppose it might just as well be me."

Dan continued to advance toward him until he was looking down into the boy's frightened eyes.

"Didn't you?" he asked.

No answer.

Dan grasped Sid by the shirt collar and held him close. Perspiration broke out on the boy's face and his shoulders began to quiver. He swallowed hard.

"Didn't you?" Dan repeated.

"Don't hit me!" he cried. "Don't hit me, you big bully!"

Dan released his grip but held Sid motionless with his eyes.

"W-w-what if I did move your scopes a little?" the boy stammered defensively. "All I did was help the god of the waterhole a little."

"I thought so," Dan said.

Seeing that he wasn't going to be hurt, Sid laughed.

"I thought it was quite a joke. Now you'll never be able to convince these Africans that their waterhole god isn't a powerful character!"

CHAPTER 6

"IT IS SAFE"

Dan turned back to the target. He adjusted the scope on his rifle and zeroed it in until he was able to center five shots in a two-inch circle. Ron and Sid watched in silence.

"That's some shooting!" Ron exclaimed approvingly. "I wish I could shoot like that!"

"You do all right. There's nothing wrong with your shooting."

Sid turned to leave, but Dan called him.

"I'm sorry I got a little rough with you, Sid. But so much is at stake in working with Ngida and Deseli that I'm afraid I lost my temper."

The boy's lips curled contemptuously.

"That's all right," he retorted. "I didn't expect your Christianity to mean any more than that."

Dan ignored the slur in his voice.

"But, Sid," he continued, and with a firmness that

was unmistakable, "don't touch either of these guns again. If you do, you'll have to answer to me! Just remember that!"

When he disappeared up the path, Dan took up the rifle Ron had been using.

"Why did you apologize to him, Danny? He deserved twice what you gave him. He could have gotten us all killed."

"I apologized because I lost my temper. A Christian shouldn't do that."

"Maybe not," Ron said, "but most guys would have pasted him one."

"I don't think he'll bother anything that belongs to us again."

He set to work on the gun.

Sid must have jammed the set screw when he changed the elevation on the scope. Dan put all his strength to it but could not move it.

"Now what's wrong?" Ron asked.

"I'm afraid he's jammed the scope so I can't move it without more tools than we have here."

He got to his feet.

"Great," Ron retorted. "That's just dandy! And now I'm without a gun!"

"Dr. Roy might be able to help us with it. And if he can't, I'm sure Mr. Sperry can when he comes back in a few days. He's got the equipment to fix almost anything."

"Just my luck," Ron grumbled. "Here we are in the best hunting I've ever been near and my gun isn't working."

They went back to the village and Dan set the crew to work. There was so much to do that both he and Ron forgot about the elephant temporarily.

The men set to work willingly, and the pile of finished boards grew. Dan selected several Africans who seemed to know the most about carpentry and set them to making door and window frames.

Toward noon Dr. Kleinschmidt came down to the place where they were working.

"How's it going?" he asked.

"Not bad," Dan answered. "Of course the work is going to slow down for a while until we teach the men to go ahead without help."

Dr. Roy watched the Africans for several minutes and nodded approvingly.

"They're doing fine," he said. "It's probably a little hard to supervise them right now when the work is so new to them, but they're doing remarkably well."

Dan glanced at his watch and halted work for noon.

"I thought you'd still be seeing patients," Ron told the doctor as the three of them walked back to the village.

"I've finished with the last of those who have to see me. There's quite a line of ulcer patients and so on, the sort of thing Coralee can tend to, but I'm about finished."

He stopped for a moment outside the rest house.

"Will you be going on this afternoon?" Dan asked.

"That's what we've been debating," Dr. Roy replied. "Coralee thinks she ought to stay here and finish taking care of these people while I go on. Then when Will and Jean come up, one of them could take her to the hospital where I'll be working."

"That would be fine," Ron said. "We'll look after her."

Dr. Roy laughed gently.

"I know she'd appreciate that, Ron. But it would sound a little strange to anyone who knows her. She's been looking after herself out here and everyone around her for the past thirty-five years."

"We'll move our beds out to the veranda," Dan put in, "and fix the rest house for Mrs. Kleinschmidt, if you decide it's best for her to stay."

"Actually, I suppose it would be best," the doctor went on. "If we can finish treating these people now there will be no need to come back for a time."

They were sitting at the dinner table when Dan saw Ngida come into the village. The young African skirted the rest house and headed for the jungle on the opposite side.

"There's Ngida," he said, pushing back from the table. "Excuse me. I've got to talk to him."

Respecting the 'Zandes' dislike of being shouted at, Dan ran after Ngida until he caught up with him.

"*Mbote*" he said, smiling.

The African stopped and set his spear on the ground.

"I have something to show you," Dan said in Lingala.

Ngida nodded and followed him back to the rest house.

"You have used a rifle, haven't you?"

"*Oui.*"

"And you know how a scope works?"

"I have used one," he said simply.

Dan called to Ron. "Bring that gun of yours here for a minute, will you?"

He took it from Ron and held it out to Ngida.

"See how the back of the scope has been raised?"

Ngida examined it carefully. "That would make it shoot high," he said.

"That's right," Dan went on. "Somebody changed the scopes purposely to deceive us."

The corners of Ngida's mouth tightened.

"So you see," Dan went on, "it wasn't the god of the waterhole who caused me to miss that elephant. It was only a man who changed the scopes."

"Maybe," the chief's son admitted, although doubt still edged his voice, "but it could be that the god of the waterhole knew we weren't going to offer him a sacrifice, so he made the person do this."

Dan straightened and ran his fingers through his close-cropped hair. What could a person do in a case like that? What could he say against that sort of logic? He prayed for guidance.

"Ngida," he began, "have I ever told you anything that was not true?"

"No," the African admitted. "You have always told us the truth. But I have only known you a few days."

"Has Will Sperry ever told you anything that wasn't true?" Dan continued. "Has Dr. Roy ever lied to you?"

Ngida thought seriously.

"No," he answered with deliberation. "They always speak the truth."

"And so do I, Ngida," Dan said. "I worship the same God they worship. The same God who tells them it is wrong to lie also guides my life. He tells me too that it is wrong to lie. I speak the truth when I say the god of the waterhole does not exist. He could not have had anything to do with changing those scopes."

The African was silent, but it seemed to Dan that his will softened a little.

"Give me one more chance to prove to you there is no waterhole god," he said. "Go with us to the waterhole once more tomorrow morning."

Fear flickered in the dark eyes.

"You say I don't lie to you. I am not lying now."

"But maybe you are mistaken," the African protested.

"The Bible tells us there is only one God," Dan repeated. "The Bible also tells the truth."

Ngida lifted his spear and began to examine it intently.

"Give me one more chance," Dan repeated. "Go with us tomorrow and see for yourself."

"I tell you tonight," he answered.

Dan watched as the youthful African turned abruptly and went striding off into the jungle.

"Now where do you suppose he's going?" he asked aloud.

A moment or two later, he told the others at the table what had happened and repeated the question.

"I'm not sure," Dr. Roy said, "but I'm guessing it has something to do with this business of going after the elephant."

"I don't understand why these people can't see how foolish their superstitions are," Ron put in. "They're beginning to get educated now."

"Education won't take paganism from a man's heart," the doctor replied. "Some of the people who have caused the most trouble for the Africans have been pagans who have been educated in some of the world's finest universities."

"That's right," Mrs. Kleinschmidt added. "The only thing that will take superstition from these people is the changed heart that comes with accepting Christ as Savior. And even then, some of them have a long, difficult time in rising above those things."

While they were talking, Ngida came out of the jungle carrying three chickens. He walked purposefully past the rest house and down the path.

"Now what do you suppose he's going to do?" Ron asked aloud.

Neither Doctor nor Mrs. Kleinschmidt answered.

Ron turned to his brother. "Would it be all right if I followed him?" he asked. "Just to see what he's going to do?"

Dan passed the question to the veteran missionaries.

"It will be all right," Dr. Roy told him.

"I'll be back as soon as I can," Ron said, getting to his feet and starting for the path.

Ron waited on the trail until Ngida was out of sight. It only took a moment or two, as the young African broke into an effortless, distance-eating trot. He was making no effort to be quiet, and Ron was able to follow him by the crackling of twigs and elephant grass.

Perspiration broke out on Ron's face and a nameless dread swept over him, stealing the strength from his powerful legs. He slowed almost imperceptibly.

Ngida had not gone far down the trail, however. He had stopped at the first round, sabi-roofed hut and was standing before it talking with a crinkled, hard-faced old African. At the sound of Ron's footsteps, the chief's son turned to face him.

"*Mbote, bwana,*" he said. There was a question in his eyes, but like most of his people he was too polite to give it voice.

The wizened old African on the ground looked up at Ron curiously.

"I–I saw you going off with the chickens," Ron stammered, "and I got curious so I–I came to see what you are going to do with them."

Ngida hesitated.

"It is nothing," he said, his eyes giving lie to the words he spoke. "It is nothing at all."

"Dr. Roy seemed to think it had something to do with whether or not you were going after the elephant with us in the morning," Ron persisted.

"It is not a sacrifice," the young African said quickly.

Ron glanced down at the old man and then up at the chief's son again.

"But it does have something to do with the hunting trip, doesn't it?"

Ngida moved uneasily.

"Some of the old men believe it is possible to divine what is going to happen," he began at last. "I don't believe it and neither does Deseli nor any of the rest of the young men, but just to see what he would say I have brought these chickens to Tala. He is going to divine for me, to tell me what will happen if we go down to the waterhole without sacrificing to the god."

Ron studied the African's face intently. Though Ngida didn't want him to know he believed in divining, the truth was written indelibly upon him.

"How does he do it?" Ron asked.

For a minute Ngida hesitated. Then, seeing that Ron was seriously interested, he spoke to Tala and turned back to the boy.

"Tala says you may stay if you wish."

"*Merci,*" Ron answered, flashing the toothless African a quick smile.

The old man got painfully to his feet and hobbled into the hut. When he came out, he was carrying a small container of liquid and a tiny, crude wooden spoon. Tala sat down cross-legged on the ground and motioned for one of the chickens.

Ngida's eyes took on a raptured look as he moved

forward and handed Tala the chicken. The old man held it tightly in his left hand, closed his eyes and began to sway a little. In a moment he began to chant in a dull monotone:

"Bengi, Bengi, you are all wise and all powerful.

"You know everything.

"You are the one who can tell us what is going to happen.

"Now we are going to ask you about Ngida."

"And Deseli," the young African whispered tautly. "Don't forget him."

"And Deseli.

"If it is safe for them to go out to the waterhole without offering a sacrifice to the god who lives there and try to kill the elephant who has been in their gardens, cause this chicken to die when I give it this potion."

Ron's heart beat faster and suddenly his mouth went dry. A chill swept over him. None of this seemed real. It was just a dream, a fantastic, horrible dream.

"What's he doing?" he whispered.

Ngida silenced him with a glance.

The old man finished his moaning chant and, picking up the spoon, dipped it in the liquid beside him and forced the chicken to swallow it.

Ngida caught his breath and crouched tensely. The chicken twitched and jerked, as though with convulsions. Then its body dropped, lifeless, to the ground.

"Ah!" Ngida exclaimed under his breath. And it seemed to Ron that some of the tension went out of his body.

But Tala was not yet finished.

"Another chicken," he ordered sternly.

Ngida handed him an emaciated little *besenji* rooster. He held it in the same manner as before.

"Bengi, Bengi, you are all wise and all powerful.

"You know everything.

"You are the one who can tell us what is going to happen.

"Now we are going to ask you once more about Ngida."

"And Deseli! Don't forget Deseli!" the African cried.

"We ask you about Ngida and Deseli.

"If it is safe for them to go out to the waterhole without offering a sacrifice to the god who lives there and try to kill the elephant who has been in their gardens, let this rooster live when I give it this potion."

Ron's eyes bugged as Tala once more dipped the spoon into the liquid and went through the ceremony of forcing the rooster to drink it.

The sprightly little rooster twisted and squirmed to free itself from Tala's grasp.

Ron stared incredulously.

The wizened African released the rooster, and it went scampering across the little clearing. For a moment it seemed as though it was going to run off into the jungle, but it stopped and began to eat, as though nothing had happened.

Ron glanced over at Ngida. A smile rested briefly on his face.

"I don't get it at all," Ron said almost in awe. "One chicken drinks that stuff and dies and the next one lives. And they both drank the same stuff."

"Of course," Ngida answered as though it was something that happened every day. "How else can we know if the divining is true?"

Before Ron could answer, Tala asked for another chicken. This time the ritual was the same as the first.

". . . If it is safe for them to go out after the elephant without sacrificing to the waterhole god, let this chicken die when I give it this potion. Then we will know that you are speaking the truth."

Ron glanced wildly about, as though almost persuaded to turn and bolt for the rest house.

Tala gave the third chicken a drink from the spoon. It died in the same way.

"I saw it," Ron muttered under his breath. "And I still don't believe it!"

Tala got to his feet and stood before Ngida.

"Bengi has spoken," he said. "It is safe for you and Deseli to go after the elephant."

"*Merci!*" Ngida exclaimed gratefully, dropping some coins into the old man's hand. "*Merci!*"

CHAPTER 7

"NOT IN SIGHT"

Back at the rest house, Ron told Dan and the Kleinschmidts what he had seen.

"Now wait a minute, Ron," his brother broke in. "You don't expect us to believe a yarn like that, do you?"

"I know it sounds crazy," Ron countered, "but it's the truth, just the same. He gave the same stuff to all three. Two of them died and one lived."

"He must have slipped something else into the stuff while you weren't looking."

"I tell you he didn't!" Ron protested. "He couldn't have. I didn't take my eyes off him for a second."

"There's got to be a trick to it," Dan said. "Things like that just don't happen."

"That's what I keep telling myself," Dr. Roy said, "but I've seen the same thing Ron is describing, and so has Coralee. If the one who was divining slipped something else into the spoon when he wanted a chicken to die, I've never been able to catch him at it."

"It's really weird," Ron continued. "It gives me the creeps just talking about it."

"There is no way of explaining many of the things that happen out here," Dr. Roy said. "I don't even try anymore."

He looked up and saw Ngida coming toward them.

"Here comes your friend," he said softly. "And unless I'm mistaken, he's going to tell you he and Deseli will go hunting with you in the morning."

The doctor was right about the purpose of the African's visit. Ngida came up to the door of the rest house and stood respectfully until Dan went out to him.

"Deseli and I will go hunting with you in the morning," he said without preliminaries. "But only one more time. We will not defy the god of the waterhole anymore."

"*Merci,* Ngida," Dan said, not mentioning the African's visit to the diviner. "You will see that there is only one God."

Ngida turned, without comment, and disappeared into the jungle.

Dr. Roy planned on leaving that afternoon, but more patients came for examination than he expected and it was almost dark by the time he finished.

"I think I'll stay and have a service this evening," he said at the supper table, "and leave the first thing in the morning."

"I think that would be better," Mrs. Kleinschmidt said. "It's so seldom anyone gets over this way that we ought to hold all the services we can while we are here."

Dan had the Africans build a large fire, and shortly after dark the service began. Mrs. Kleinschmidt played an accordion accompaniment, and the native pastor led them as they sang a few songs.

Dr. Roy leaned over to Dan and whispered, "Do you recognize the tune?"

"Just barely," he said.

"They only have a five-note scale," the doctor went on, "so their singing sounds like a monotone to us, but they love to sing. And when they are taught our scale and part-singing, their voices are beautiful."

They drew back their heads and sang loudly; and when one number was finished they called for another. At last the pastor closed the singing with prayer and turned over the meeting to Dr. Kleinschmidt.

He got to his feet purposefully and moved closer to the fire. A tall, lean-faced man, he seemed even more frail in the flickering light of the dancing flames. The deep brown of his forehead contrasted with the white of his hair.

The Africans quieted expectantly. For an instant or two the speaker paused while two young Africans approached the fire and sat down. Ron glanced up at them and caught his breath.

Ngida and Deseli! And the Kleinschmidts said they seldom came!

Once everyone was seated and quiet, Dr. Roy began to speak. He spoke with quiet dignity in the 'Zandes' native tongue. Although Dan and Ron could only understand a few words, they could tell by watching the intent faces that they were clinging to each word.

Ron looked over at the chief's sons. They were serious too. As serious as they had been out at the waterhole when Dan missed the elephant. Ron prayed silently that God would speak to their hearts through Dr. Roy.

When the speaker finished and closed in prayer, a hush settled over the little group. For several minutes the 'Zandes sat in silence. Then, by ones and twos they got to their feet and disappeared into the darkness. Ngida and Deseli were among the first to leave.

"You were really getting through to them, Dr. Roy," Dan said. "I could tell by watching them."

"I noticed that too," Coralee Kleinschmidt said. "And Ngida and Deseli were here. Isn't that wonderful?"

"Yes," the doctor said in the same soft voice he used in his message. "It was wonderful to see them at our service. We've been praying for them so very long."

"I wanted to talk with them," Dan said, "but they got away before I had a chance."

"That's the way it always is," Mrs. Kleinschmidt said. "They seldom come to the meetings, and when they do they clear out before we have an opportunity to talk with them."

"We'll have to keep praying for them," Ron said.

Mrs. Kleinschmidt brushed at her hair.

"That's what we always say," she answered. "And I know that's true. But there are times when it is very discouraging. We've been praying for them so long."

"Yes," her husband said, "the pagan practices are very strong in their lives."

"Maybe we'll have a chance to do a little more with them after tomorrow," Dan said, "after they see there's nothing to this god of the waterhole who has them so terribly frightened."

The following morning Dan checked his rifles with care and he and Ron got ready to go out after the elephant, while Dr. Kleinschmidt supervised the packing of his truck and his wife cooked the breakfast.

The sun was not yet up when Dr. Roy drove out of the village toward the Sudan border.

"How long do you plan on staying?" Ron asked Mrs. Kleinschmidt.

"There's enough here to keep me busy for a week," she said, bustling around the veranda. "But I think I'll be able to take care of everyone who needs immediate treatment in a couple of days. Roy said he would be back for me as soon as he could if Will and Jean don't get back."

Sid appeared at the rest house first that morning, followed shortly by Ngida and Deseli and the other Africans.

"I thought maybe you had changed your mind, Dan," Sid said, his voice laced with contempt. "Or are you going to wait until you get out to the waterhole to lose your nerve?"

Dan glanced up at him and grinned.

"If you're afraid to go along," he said, "you're welcome to stay at home."

"I would have stayed at home," the boy retorted, "believe me. But this time I brought my own gun. I don't have to depend on you!"

Ron looked at him quickly.

"What about the license?"

"Suppose you let me worry about the license."

They walked on for several minutes.

"What I want to know," Sid began again, "is how did you get the boys to come along today? They hardly act scared this morning."

"They aren't scared."

"Don't tell me you got them to believe that stuff you've been trying to feed them."

"I wish we could claim credit for it," Dan said, "but the truth is that Ngida went to a diviner who told him that they would not be hurt if they went with us after the elephant without sacrificing to the god of the waterhole."

Sid laughed raucously.

"I didn't think you'd get them to forget the old ways. It's going to take more than talk to get those two to become Christians."

He seemed relieved that Ngida and Deseli had not made a profession of faith, and he whistled tunelessly as they walked along. He whistled, that is, until Ngida stopped and looked back disapprovingly.

"You'd better stop whistling," Dan whispered to him. "We're getting close to the waterhole."

"Okay, okay! But you're not going to get anything. Remember, you haven't made a sacrifice yet."

The little group had been comparatively quiet ever since they left the village, but now a hush settled over them and they glided forward stealthily.

The Africans made no sound at all, their bare feet sliding noiselessly over the rough stubble. And the Orlises and Sid walked as quietly as possible in their tennis shoes.

Someone would step on a dry twig or shoot of elephant grass with a telltale crackle. The Africans would stare at him, and occasionally stop for an instant in a silent plea for quiet, but they were too polite to say anything.

The pace slowed as they neared the waterhole and the tension mounted. They crouched and moved forward from one clump of elephant grass to another.

"Maybe we ought to give up," Sid said uncertainly. "It's spooky out here."

Even as he spoke Ngida froze and pointed with a trembling finger.

"Elephant!" he managed.

The word went from one to another in a breathless whisper.

The elephant was still at the waterhole!

Ron's throat constricted until he could scarcely breathe, and he clenched his teeth to keep them from chattering.

Dan reached back and took his rifle from the gun bearer. His experienced eye ran over the weapon critically. The scope had not been touched since he readjusted it. He made sure of that. And the safety was on. He pulled the bolt noiselessly and noted that the big rifle was loaded with steel-jacketed ammunition.

Everything was ready.

He took a quick, backward glance at the Africans behind him. Their faces were strained and drawn, and their eyes reflected the terror that must have gripped their hearts. Briefly, Dan remembered what Dr. Roy had said about them.

"O God," he prayed silently as he began to move forward, "quiet their hearts and help them not to panic."

Ngida moved quietly to one side to allow Dan to pass.

"Be careful, *bwana,*" he whispered in Lingala. "That elephant is a bad one."

"We'll get him," Dan answered.

He motioned to the others to stay where they were and moved skillfully through the brush to his right. The elephant stood still feeding in the tall grass. Then he would stop to listen. When he did so Dan stood motionless until the animal resumed eating once more.

Sneaking up on the elephant was very similar to hunting deer on the Angle. As Dan maneuvered closer to the big animal, he recalled all the things his dad taught him about stalking game. It took longer to move close to the elephant than he had thought it would, but at last he was within 30 yards. He inched to one side to avoid a small branch and started to bring his rifle to his shoulder.

Then the wind died down and changed suddenly. The elephant caught the scent of Ngida and the others! His trunk went up like a sentinel, writhing as it tested the hated scent on the wind. Great ears fanned out and quivered nervously.

All sound at the waterhole suspended momentarily. Dan flicked off the safety and started to squeeze the trigger.

Without warning the elephant trumpeted and threw back his head. For an instant Dan lost him in the scope.

Then everything happened at once!

The Africans turned and ran, their bare feet making a fierce beat on the dry ground as they scrambled for safety.

Ngida screamed! A wild, terrifying scream!

Dan whirled, his rifle still at his shoulder.

A huge buffalo that must have been lying in the grass had been infuriated by the vibration set up by the running of the natives. He leaped to his feet and charged blindly in their direction.

And Ngida, frozen in terror, stood motionless, directly in the maddened animal's path!

Dan lowered his rifle on the buffalo and would have pulled the trigger, but he could not! Ngida was in the line of fire!

"Shoot!" Dan shouted to Sid. "Shoot!"

But the other hunter was not in sight.

Dan scrambled to one side and fired. His bullet caught the buffalo a glancing blow and the ugly creature veered slightly, enough to throw him off balance.

Nevertheless one wicked, curved horn caught Ngida in the abdomen and tossed him aside. Dan worked the bolt of his rifle frantically and fired again. The buffalo staggered almost to his knees, caught himself, and dashed off into the jungle.

Ngida was sprawled grotesquely on the ground!

CHAPTER 8

DRIVER ANTS TO THE RESCUE

At the first report of the rifle, the elephant turned quickly and ran into the jungle with surprising speed. But Dan gave no thought to that beast. Nor did he think of the wounded buffalo that went staggering into the jungle near the spot where Ngida lay.

Instead he hurried to the injured African and knelt beside him.

"Ngida!" he said softly. "Ngida!"

The chief's young son opened his pain-dulled eyes and moved his lips, but no sound came out.

"Ngida," Dan whispered once more.

Ron ran out beside him.

"How is he?" he asked breathlessly.

Dan examined Ngida quickly. He had a long, ugly tear in his stomach, just below the belt line of his tattered shorts.

"That's bad, isn't it?" Ron whispered.

Dan nodded.

"I don't know how bad," he said, "but any injury in this part of the body is bad."

"I'd have shot that buffalo," Ron protested miserably, "but I didn't have my gun!"

By this time the Africans and Sid came running back. Sid was the first to reach them, followed closely by Deseli.

"Why didn't you shoot him, Orlis?" Sid blustered. "Why did you wait until he got to Ngida?"

"We'll talk about that later," Dan answered. "Right now we've got to get help for him, and pronto, or it's going to be too late."

"If he dies," Deseli exclaimed, his voice rasping with hatred, "you are the one who's responsible, *Bwana* Orlis. You will have killed him because you dared to defy the god of the waterhole."

"We'll talk about that when the sun goes down," Dan said, using a phrase of Will Sperry's.

He stood and looked over the ragged group of frightened, almost hostile Africans.

"You," he exclaimed, pointing to one, "run back to the village and get Madame Kleinschmidt, quick! Tell her what happened and bring her out here just as fast as you can!"

The African would have started immediately, but as he turned to go Dan stopped him.

"I'd better send a note with you," he said, "so there'll be no mistake."

Ron wrote the note hastily while Dan spoke to the Africans.

"Now," he continued decisively, "who have bicycles?"

Almost every hand went up.

Dan hesitated, looking them over carefully.

"I want you to go after the doctor," he said, picking out a strong, alert young man. "Take this note to Madame Kleinschmidt and she will tell you how to reach the doctor. And give this note to Dr. Roy."

In a moment both of the Africans were gone, running as fast as they could.

"What are we going to do?" Ron asked. "Wait here until Mrs. Kleinschmidt and the doctor get here?"

Dan pressed his lips together thoughtfully.

"I don't like the looks of this at all," he said, keeping his voice low, even though he was speaking English and the Africans could not understand what he was saying. "I believe we'd better make a stretcher and carry him up the trail to meet Mrs. Kleinschmidt. We can save time that way."

Sid was still standing there, white-faced and shaken.

"He'll die, Dan," he said in desperation. "And then they'll blame us! There's no telling what they might do!"

"Better get your shirt off, Ron," Dan told Ron as he took off his own. "We're going to need both to make a stretcher."

"We've got to get out of here while he's still alive," Sid went on, his voice rising hysterically. "If you run over an African out here, you're not supposed to stop because the authorities are afraid of what the villagers might do to you. You're supposed to go to the nearest commissioner and get soldiers to go back with you. I tell you it's not safe for us to stay here! They'll blame us for whatever happens."

"You can go if you want to," Dan said firmly, "but we're not going to leave him. That's for sure."

They got two long poles, put them through the sleeves of the shirts, fastened the buttons and laid the improvised stretcher on the ground beside Ngida. Carefully they moved the injured African onto it.

Sid hung back as though he wanted to leave but could not quite bring himself to do so.

The chief's son was awake and wanted to talk to Dan.

"I cannot understand it, *bwana*" he said. "Bengi said it was safe to come here, and he's never been wrong before."

"It is because of the god of the waterhole," Deseli broke in, his dark eyes fixed accusingly on Dan. "The god of the waterhole is stronger than Bengi. He is more powerful than any other god."

Dan did not challenge him. There wasn't time.

"We'd better get started for the village," he said. "Ngida needs medical attention as soon as possible."

Deseli moved closer to Dan.

"If he dies, *bwana*," he said darkly, his usually mild voice charged with emotion, "it will be because you made him come to the waterhole without sacrificing to the god. His death will be on you.

"We'll talk about that after we get help for Ngida," Dan told him.

At his direction four Africans picked up the chief's son on the stretcher and moved carefully along the rough, narrow trail.

A groan escaped Ngida's lips and Deseli winced and glared at Danny.

"I don't care what you do," Sid said, taking his gun from the bearer. "I'm going to get out of here now while I've still got the chance!"

An instant later he was gone.

Ron and Dan both prayed silently each step of the way. Not for their own safety but for the young man who was so badly hurt.

They had covered almost a mile when they met Mrs. Kleinschmidt on the trail. With her were two young Africans. Her cheeks were flecked with per-spiration and her breathing was short and labored.

"I'm so glad you started this way," she said, panting. "When I read your note, I got my things together and came as fast as I could, but I was afraid I might be too late."

She looked down at the one who had been gored by the buffalo.

"Why, it's Ngida!" she exclaimed, kneeling down beside him. "Open my bag."

She spoke softly, but with authority. Both Dan and Ron jumped to do as she ordered.

She examined the wound hurriedly and took a syringe from her case, filling it with morphine.

"First of all, we've got to do something to ease the pain," she said.

"How badly is he hurt?" Dan whispered.

"Critically, I'm afraid," she answered. "The intestine is ripped. Doctor has had many cases like this in the years we've been out here. A torn intestine must be repaired within an hour of the injury or–" Her voice died away significantly.

"An hour?" Ron echoed. "It's already been more than thirty minutes."

"How long will it take for Dr. Roy to get here?" Dan wanted to know.

"Too long," she said. "I've got to try to take care of it myself."

She went through her bag carefully.

"There's nothing here for a suture!" she exclaimed. "I don't even have any thread!"

"I could unravel one of my socks!" Ron offered.

"The thread in your sock wouldn't be strong enough or sterile," she countered.

Her lips went together tightly.

"Surely there's something we can do, isn't there?" Dan asked.

She was a long while in answering.

"Years ago," she began hesitantly, "Roy had this same thing happen and he had to perform an emergency operation."

She paused.

"It just might work at that." She turned to Deseli

and spoke hurriedly in 'Zande. "Have the boys get me as many driver ants as they can! And hurry! We must have them to save Ngida's life!"

"Right away!" Deseli cried. "They are everywhere!"

In a few minutes the Africans began to return with the ants, held gingerly in bark cones.

"Good!" Mrs. Kleinschmidt said.

By this time the morphine had begun to take hold. Ngida began to relax a little and his breathing became more uniform and easy.

She examined the tear in the intestine carefully and worked the tough skin into place with her fingers.

"Get me the tweezers," she ordered crisply, "and don't think I'm crazy. The pioneer doctors out here used driver ants for sutures once in a while."

While the Orlises stared at her incredulously, she picked up a large driver ant with the tweezers. Then she lowered it painstakingly to the tear made by the buffalo's horn. The long, powerful pincers dug deeply into either side of the opening and clamped the skin firmly together.

"Ah!" Mrs. Kleinschmidt said, pulling the ant's body from the head to leave the pincers imbedded there. And without wasting a moment she took another ant, and still another, and repeated the process.

"If I wasn't seeing this," Dan said, more to himself than anyone else, "I'd scarcely believe it."

"It's surprising how well they work," Mrs. Kleinschmidt said without looking up. "Actually they are something like the clamps Roy uses for many of his operations now, only of course they're a great deal smaller."

She finished with the tear in the intestine and finally began to close the wound.

"I was hoping Roy would get here to take a look at this before the skin is closed," she said, "but we can't wait for him. The boy may have had difficulty finding him, or they may have had car trouble coming back. We'll have to do the best we can."

She worked patiently, and in about fifteen minutes she had finished. The Africans standing around watched in silence. They glanced at Dan now and again, sullenly, but still did not speak.

Ron stepped closer and looked down at Ngida. The nurse had not had a proper anesthetic for such an operation and Ngida's young body was twisted and racked with pain. His face was beaded with moisture and his mouth worked wordlessly. His hands, on each side of the litter, clutched at the ground until the cords stood out on the backs in bold relief.

"He's in so much pain," Ron said. "Isn't there something you can give him?"

"I have a little more morphine," Mrs. Kleinschmidt said. "I'll give that to him as soon as I dare."

Ron looked at Ngida and then up at the nurse. "Do—do you think he will live?" he asked.

"I—I just don't know, Ron," she said. "With every breath I've taken I've been praying that he would."

"We've been praying too."

"It's the first time I've ever done anything like this," she continued. "And I wouldn't have done it now except there was nothing else to do."

After the wound had been sewed, Ngida began to rest a bit easier. Mrs. Kleinschmidt took his pulse.

"It's beginning to slow down a little," she said.

Deseli came over to her.

"My brother," he began–"he will be all right?"

"We are praying God that he will."

"If *Bwana* Orlis had not made us go down to the waterhole," he began, his voice harsh with anger, "the god of the waterhole would not have become angry and Ngida would not have been hurt."

"You know that is not true," she answered. "Dr. Roy and I have defied your gods for years. They would have killed us long ago if there was anything to them."

Deseli thought about that for a moment.

"All I know," he said at last, "is that Ngida was never hurt before *Bwana* Orlis took us down to the waterhole without making the sacrifice. Our fathers have told us of the god there. Now we have seen how powerful he is."

She tried to reason with him, but it was no use. He refused to believe differently. Dan listened help-lessly while they talked.

Despair swept over him. He had been trying so hard to lead the chief's sons to Christ. He had prayed so often.

Mrs. Kleinschmidt resumed her vigil beside her patient. An hour passed and an hour and a half.

"His pulse is still dropping," she said. "I think I'll give him the rest of the morphine and have him moved to the village. Roy ought to be along by the time we get back."

At her direction, the Africans picked up Ngida with great care and once more started for the village. His youthful face twisted momentarily with pain. They carried him tenderly, walking much slower than before, to keep from jouncing him. Gradually the effects of the morphine dulled the pain, and he closed his eyes drowsily. He did not open them again until they reached the village.

"Dr. Roy isn't here," Ron said, looking about. "It's a good thing you took care of Ngida's wound."

She nodded.

"I've seen too many unavoidable delays out here," she said, "to wait on something as critical as that."

The litter-bearers stopped and looked at her questioningly.

"We'll have to make the rest house into a hospital room," she told Dan and Ron without a moment's hesitation. "Ngida will have to be close by, so Roy can examine him and keep a close eye on him for a while."

"That's all right," Dan answered. "We can sleep on the veranda or anywhere."

They moved their things out of the rest house and helped Mrs. Kleinschmidt get Ngida into bed and rig the mosquito net over him. Deseli went to tell his father what had happened.

Only then did the aging nurse appear tired. She sat down in a chair, wearily, and wiped the perspiration from her forehead.

"If you want to rest," Dan said quickly, "Ron and I will watch Ngida."

She shook her head.

"I'm all right," she said. "It's just that I get a little tired after an ordeal like this. I can't walk quite as far as I used to."

The sound of a roaring motor drowned her words.

"Dr. Roy!" Ron cried, leaping to his feet.

CHAPTER 9

"RIGHT ON TOP OF US"

The gray-haired doctor got out of his truck and walked toward the rest house. His wife and the Orlises met him at the door.

"I came as soon as I could. What's wrong?"

"It's Ngida," Mrs. Kleinschmidt said. "He was gored by a buffalo. I took care of him the best I could."

The doctor went into the rest house and began to examine the young patient.

"M-m-m-m," he said, noting the driver ants his wife had used in the place of sutures or clamps. "I had almost forgotten how we used to use those ants."

"I had to, Roy," she said. "I didn't have anything else and he had to be sewed up right away."

He took Ngida's pulse and temperature.

"I couldn't have done a better job myself, Coralee. I'm proud of you."

Dan saw that she looked desperately tired and began to realize what a strain had been on her.

"Just the same, I'm glad you're here, Roy," she told him.

"You'd better go and lie down, my dear."

Before she could leave, Deseli and a wizened, arthritic 'Zande came hobbling to the rest house.

"*Mbote,*" Dr. Roy said, smiling in greeting.

The old chief greeted him soberly.

"I have come to see my son."

Dr. Roy and Ngida's father disappeared into the rest house. Deseli, who remained at the door, glared at Dan and Ron.

Ron shivered under the icy stare.

"I didn't know anyone could hate as much as Deseli hates us," he said.

"That's only because he does not know the Lord as his Savior."

Dan went over to Dr. Roy's truck and stood there for a moment or two.

"Ron," he said at last, "I just thought of something we've got to do."

"Like finishing the doors and windows we started?" Ron asked.

Dan shook his head.

"It's something more pressing than that. We left a wounded buffalo down by that waterhole. And a wounded buffalo is as dangerous as any animal in the jungle. He can kill somebody if we don't go down and shoot him."

Ron swallowed hard.

"I suppose that's right," he said, "but after seeing what that old guy did to Ngida I don't know whether I want to tangle with him or not."

"I was figuring on going after him alone," Dan said.

"Oh, no, you don't! I'm going along."

"But we've only got one gun that's usable."

"I don't care about that," Ron protested. "You're not going down there without me."

Dan got his rifle, removed the steel-jacketed bullets and replaced them with lead. Deseli watched them curiously.

"This time the god of the waterhole will be satisfied with nothing less than death," he said in Lingala. "He gave us a last warning when Ngida was hurt."

Dan stuffed his pockets full of ammunition.

"We've got to get that wounded buffalo," he explained. "He is apt to kill someone if we don't."

"No one will go with you," Deseli said, as though that would settle the matter. "If you go, you will have to go alone."

"That's what we planned to do. We've been there before. There's no chance of our getting lost."

Deseli stared at him in silence.

They left the village, crossed the road, and went into the elephant grass on the other side. By this time it was late afternoon and the setting sun was casting long shadows before them.

"Do you suppose those buffaloes are really as mean and dangerous as everyone says they are?" Ron asked.

"I don't know about that," Dan answered, "but from all I've heard they don't exactly make good pets."

The Orlises had only gone a few steps when a familiar voice called to them.

"Dan! Ron! Wait a jiffy!"

They turned to see Sid hurrying through the elephant grass toward them.

"Hi," they said, greeting him.

Sid stopped beside them. His face was flushed from running and there was a strange look in his eyes.

"I want to talk to you for a minute."

"Sure thing," Dan answered. Then he glanced at the lowering sun. "Only we're in a hurry. We want to get down to the waterhole and kill that wounded buffalo before he hurts someone else."

"You–you mean you're going out after that guy?" Sid asked incredulously. "After what he did to Ngida?"

"Somebody has to destroy him," Dan said simply, "or he'll kill someone."

Sid shifted from one foot to another uneasily. "I–I wanted to explain what h-h-happened at the waterhole this morning," he went on. "I–I was going to shoot the buffalo but my g-g-gun wouldn't work. I–I mean it j-j-jammed."

Dan noted the hesitation in his voice and the look of guilt in his eyes, but he said nothing.

"Ngida is going to get well," he said. "That's the main thing."

Sid swallowed hard.

"I–I just didn't want you to think I–I got scared a-a-and ran away like the Africans," he went on.

"It wouldn't be anything to be ashamed of, if you had," Dan said. "It's the sort of thing that could happen to any of us."

Ron took half a step down the path.

"Don't you think we'd better get on our way, Dan?" he asked. "It's going to be dark before long."

"I suppose we had."

Dan turned back to Sid. "Want to go along?"

"Oh, no!" he retorted quickly. "Not me! I saw enough of that buffalo to last me for a long time!"

Dan started on but paused.

"Sid," he began quietly, "did you ever stop to think that there is something much more dangerous than that wounded buffalo?"

"What is it?" Sid asked, his lips curling contemptuously. "Another buffalo?"

Dan shook his head.

"Neglecting the Lord Jesus Christ," he continued, "and the salvation He alone can give."

Sid started.

"Christ pleads with each of us to confess our sin and put our trust in Him," Dan pressed, "but it's up to us whether we accept Him, reject Him, or just ignore Him."

"I might have known you'd try to preach to me!" the boy retorted, his voice rising. "I'm getting along all right just as I am!"

"That's what Ngida thought before that buffalo jumped out of the grass and took after him," Dan said. "None of us knows how long we're going to live. It may be a long while or it may not. If we haven't confessed our sin and taken a stand for Christ before something happens to us it will be too late. There is no other chance!"

Sid's face paled, and for a long minute he stood there, wavering in his decision. Then his face steeled.

"You don't need to think you can scare me into it," he snapped. "I'm not falling for that old line."

Dan would have continued, but the boy started back for the road abruptly.

"And don't think I'm not going with you to the waterhole because I'm scared to go," he called over his shoulder. "It's just that I've got a lot of work to do at home."

When he was out of sight Ron said, "I feel sort of sick inside. Sid was close to making a decision for Christ."

Dan nodded. "I feel the same way."

They started in the direction of the waterhole. "You know, there are a lot of guys and girls like that. They hear the way of salvation and want to become Christians. Some of them get so close you almost feel as though you could accept Christ for them, but they determine not to yield to Him, so they go on their merry way, as Sid did just now."

"And there may not be another chance," Ron added.

"Exactly," Dan said. "That's what is so sad about it."

They stopped talking as they neared the waterhole.

"That buffalo went charging off into the jungle," Ron whispered. "Won't we have to track him down?"

"Maybe," Dan answered, "and maybe not. He might have turned and come back to the waterhole. You can never tell what a wounded animal will do."

He stopped, checked his rifle mechanically, and began to move forward, his finger on the safety.

"Whatever you do, Ron," he breathed tensely, "keep your eyes open. If that buffalo charges us, we may have only a split second to–"

His voice choked off.

There was a bellow of rage to their right! Two dozen yards away, a huge black hulk came rising out of the *sabi* grass and charged them!

"The buffalo!" Ron cried.

Dan slammed his heavy rifle to his shoulder, squinted coolly into the scope and squeezed the trigger! The buffalo staggered and almost dropped to his knees.

"You hit him!"

But the maddened animal was not down! He righted himself and came on, head down, bellowing defiance.

In one smooth, quick movement Dan opened the bolt to eject the empty brass casing and force another cartridge into the barrel. Again he shot.

The bull buffalo slowed, but somehow managed to stay on his feet and keep coming, his wicked horns in battle position. Dan squeezed the trigger a third time, working the gun action with lightning speed, and shot again before the reverberations had died away.

The last time he shot, only the buffalo's ugly head was visible in the scope. He was so close. He took another step or two toward them and collapsed, almost at Dan's and Ron's feet.

Ron wiped the perspiration from his forehead and expelled his breath slowly.

"Wow!" he cried when he could speak once more. "I didn't think that buffalo was ever going down! They can sure soak up the lead!"

Dan examined the big animal carefully to be sure he would not get up again. Then he grinned.

"He looked as big as a freight train and twice as ugly," he said, "when I drew a bead on him through the scope the last time. I thought he was right on top of us."

"Let me clue you in," Ron said. "He was."

"Well," Dan replied, "he's not going to injure anyone else. That's for sure."

"We can thank God your last bullet hit his brain," Ron ventured. "It could have been rough if you'd missed him."

"I'm afraid so." Dan checked the dark skin for bullet holes.

"Here's where I hit him when he was charging Ngida, and here are the other shots. Any one of them would have killed him – in time."

"That's just what we were fresh out of," Ron answered. "Time! He could have really made a mess of us while we were waiting for one of those bullets to do him in."

"He's not going to hurt anyone else," Dan said. "That's the main thing."

They were still standing there when there was a sudden movement in the grass behind them and Deseli stepped out.

"Deseli!" Ron exclaimed.

He stared down at the dead buffalo.

"He–he didn't kill you," he observed, a strange new tone in his voice.

"No," Dan answered. "He did not kill us. And we are at the waterhole." The last he added significantly.

"*Oui.*" Deseli walked around the buffalo, still incredulous.

"He was a bad one," he said, as though he were talking to himself, "but you killed him."

"We killed him," Dan repeated simply, "and we did not make a sacrifice to your waterhole god."

Deseli acted as though he had not heard.

"I'm surprised to see you here," Ron ventured, to break the silence. "You told us a little while ago that you were afraid to come to the waterhole."

"Only with you," the young African said truthfully. "I did not come to hunt. I only came to see what happened to you."

"And you found that nothing happened to us," Dan went on. "How do you account for that, Deseli?"

The African shrugged.

"Your God warred with the god of the waterhole," he said, "and overpowered him. Your God is very powerful."

"That is what we have been trying to tell you," Dan said. "The God we worship is the living God. He is the One who made the world and everything in it. And He tells us that we must have no other gods before Him."

Deseli's entire manner was different.

"We will talk of Him again," he said, "but now we must get back to the village. The people will want to carry the meat in before the jackals and the leopards find it."

CHAPTER 10

"THEY STOOD THEIR GROUND"

Dan and Ron and Deseli hurried back to the village, and the chief's son got the men to go back with him for the buffalo meat.

"But what of the god of the waterhole?" one of them demanded. "What will he do to us?"

Deseli stared at him.

"The god of the waterhole is dead."

"Do you want us to go along?" Dan asked. "We can take the rifle and go with you if you'd like."

Deseli shook his head.

"No, *bwana*. We are not afraid anymore."

While Dan was talking to the chief's son, Ron walked quietly into the rest house.

"How's Ngida?" he whispered.

"He's resting very quietly," Mrs. Kleinschmidt said. "In fact we were talking to him a few minutes ago."

"We've been praying for him all the time."

"And so have we." Then she changed the subject abruptly. "What happened out there this evening? And why are Deseli and the others going back?"

Briefly Ron told her what had taken place.

Her eyes lighted.

"That could be the break we've been looking and praying for," she said.

Dan and Ron waited up an hour past their normal Congo bedtime, hoping they would have a chance to talk with Deseli when he and the others returned. But they were so long in getting back that they finally gave up and went to bed.

The next morning when they awakened the sun was high above the horizon.

"Are you two ever going to get out of bed?" Mrs. Kleinschmidt called to them good-naturedly. "I'm not going to hold breakfast much longer."

"We'll be right with you," Dan answered.

He and Ron got out of their beds and went into the rest house to dress.

Ngida was lying there, eyes open, and Deseli was crouched beside him. So intent were they in conversation that neither of them noticed the Orlises.

". . . And they stood their ground," Deseli was saying in Lingala, "and kept shooting until the buffalo dropped at their very feet!"

"The other one ran away," Ngida said, speaking

of Sidney Rucker. "He could have shot the buffalo before he got to me, but he turned and ran."

"He is different than these two," Deseli went on. He breathed deeply. "It is that God of theirs. He is the One who makes them different!"

"*Oui,*" Dan broke in. "Our God is the One who makes us different."

He went over to the bed and sat down on one corner.

"Ron and I are just as Sidney Rucker," he went on, "except for the strength God gives us."

He paused momentarily so they could grasp the full meaning of what he had said.

"W-w-would He give us that strength?" Ngida asked.

"He will give you something more important than courage or strength," Dan went on. "He will give you eternal life, if you will only take it."

He outlined the plan of salvation as simply and as carefully as he knew how. He told them how God sent His Son to earth, how He lived, and died, and rose again.

"And all for one purpose," he concluded, "and only one purpose. So that we could be saved by confessing our sin and putting our trust in Him for eternal life."

The young Africans turned that over in their minds.

"That is the same thing *Bwana* Sperry and Doctor Roy have been telling us," Ngida said at last. "But we didn't believe it. The old ways–"

"The old ways bring fear," Dan went on. "Wouldn't you like to be free of fear?"

The young Africans were silent.

"The Lord Jesus Christ can free you of fear of the evil spirits and the taboos of your fathers. He can give you eternal life if you will only confess your sin and put your trust in Him."

Dan continued to talk calmly. At last Ngida stopped him.

"I want to be a Christian," he said quietly.

"And so do I," Deseli put in.

The chief's sons and the Orlises bowed their heads and Dan guided them in a simple prayer of repentance. Mrs. Kleinschmidt and her doctor husband stood in the door of the rest house, bowing their heads in a silent prayer of thanksgiving.

* * *

That evening Will and Jean Sperry came back to the village in their heavily loaded pickup.

"Well," the big missionary said, "the vacation is over. We just stopped at the kiln and the bricks are ready. We'll start hauling them in the morning.

"That is good news," Dan replied. "I've been wondering what we would do when we finished the windows and doors."

"You aren't going to be lying around," Mr. Sperry said. "That's for sure."

"Something happened this morning that is more important than getting the hospital started," Mrs. Kleinschmidt broke in. Briefly she told them of the god of the waterhole, Ngida getting hurt, and finally of the salvation of both the chief's sons.

"That's wonderful!" Jean Sperry exclaimed. "We've been praying for them for years."

Ron and Dan looked at one another and smiled broadly. It was strange, and somehow very wonderful, that God had given them the privilege of dealing with Ngida and Deseli.

Ron turned and looked toward the village. But that was only one victory – a very small one. That was all it could be when so many, many others around them were in darkness and lost without a Savior.

An ache began to grow in his heart. There was so much to be done for Christ in Africa. So very much! And so few were burdened to do it!

THE DANNY ORLIS SERIES

The Danny Orlis series, by Bernard Palmer, delivers a blend of adventure, mystery, and suspense through various settings—from the Canadian wilderness to Guatemalan jungles. Danny Orlis, an adept outdoorsman, skilled athlete, and committed Christian, employs his quick thinking, calm bravery, and biblical solutions to confront everyday problems and hair-raising dangers. Early stories focus on Danny navigating school life, sports, and outdoor challenges, while in later books, Danny and his wife Kay provide wisdom and guidance to youngsters facing lifelike situations and challenges. Having sold over two million copies, this series has made Palmer a renowned author in Christian youth literature. Palmer is also the author of the Felicia Cartright series and various other series for Christian youth.

AVAILABLE FROM WWW.ANEKOPRESS.COM

www.ingramcontent.com/pod-product-compliance
Lightning Source LLC
Chambersburg PA
CBHW070912100726
47907CB00008B/2287